PANAMA'S GOLD
A TALE OF GREED

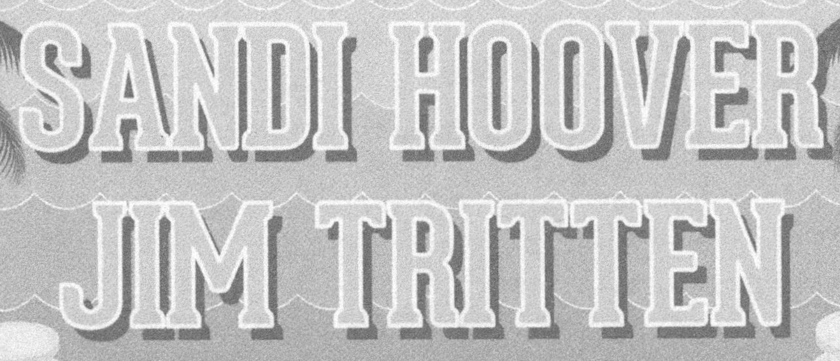

SANDI HOOVER
JIM TRITTEN

Panama's Gold

Copyright © 2021 by Sandi Hoover, LLC

Published by Red Penguin Books

Bellerose Village, New York

Library of Congress Control Number: 2021917567

ISBN

Print 978-1-63777-312-3

Digital 978-1-63777-313-0

CONTENTS

PROLOGUE – ISTHMUS OF PANAMA 1882

Pierre's shoulders sagged. Sweat burned his eyes. The rips in his shirt matched bloody streaks on his skin. Blisters on his hands wept, rubbed raw by dragging the survey rod with its heavy metal chain. He had thrown away his shredded, rotten gloves earlier that day. Following an overgrown stream bed at the base of a dormant volcano, engineers planned for the dredging of a ship canal.

Shit! Not what I expected from the Compagnie Universelle du Canal Interocéanique. They lied. Beaches and crystal water like one of those Caribbean isles—hah. Plenty of money to spend on the señoritas—hah. With my luck? Should've known it was too good.

A sharp whistle stopped him, and he pulled the chain taut again. Pierre held the pole for the surveyor's reading. Another signal said the measurement was taken and released him from his momentary pose. He pounded a stake into the ground, then fumbled a large metal nail from a bag hung on his shoulders. Pierre looked around for a place to fasten it, where the rest of the crew would find it. Four swift strikes with his mallet embedded the spike near eye level in a tree with peeling white bark. His final act was tying a strip of red flagging on the nail and stake. More shrill whistles indicated time for a break.

Pierre had already dropped his pole and markers when Maurice hurried up. Maurice grimaced as he stumbled over cut branches on the path. "My God! I nearly sliced my leg on this machete. Today is hot enough to melt this blade." Maurice wiped the sweat from his brow with the sleeve of his shirt. "Water's gone, so I'll refill my bag. Here's the machete. It's time to trade jobs when I return."

Pierre pressed his water container hard against his cracked lips, waving his hand to indicate he heard what Maurice had said. As he lowered his drink, something caught his eye. *What's that?* Pierre tipped his head again. The tiny bright gleam was only visible from one angle. He saw it once more and pushed his way off the trail. *Lost it. No, there it is. What? That doesn't belong here.* Lured by the glimmer of a shiny something, he fought his way through the dense woods. Each footstep was a struggle since he had left the machete in the pile of equipment. After detouring around a snag, he realigned himself with the glint and pressed on. It was only fifteen or twenty feet, but it could have been a kilometer, as hard as it was to navigate, with the trail disappearing behind him.

The errant shaft of light left the shiny object, but Pierre had its location identified by some of the strange vegetation in the steaming jungle. He climbed over a drooping vine and was suddenly within arm's reach of his goal. Peering at it, he gasped. *An old-looking battered gold coin! Nailed here?* Pierre examined all the trees he could see from his position, stepped back, and turned in a slow circle. *Aha! One more, what's this?* He pulled another vine out of the way, disturbing ants that ran up his arm and bit viciously. "Shit!" He swiped at them, and dancing in pain knocked his shin on something sharp. Pierre's unprotected hands dripped with blood and sweat.

"What?" He yanked at the vines and leaves shielding his view until he could make out a portion of a solid metallic object. *Makes no sense.* The angled edge of an ornately designed corner protector jutted out at knee height. Vine-covered wooden slats were attached to the metal corner. Almost all the boards had rotted and collapsed inside the remnants of a box. He wrapped his hand with a handkerchief and pulled away a couple of disintegrating pieces and froze—his mouth falling open in shock. Gold coins, golden figurines, necklaces, earrings, and objects he couldn't identify. He reached in and extracted a single coin and a small figure. *Ouch, such a headache. My eyes hurt. Money, not French. Much older than me. The figure…Damn whistles. Damn foreman—shit. If I leave it here, I will not have to share anything. Those others…don't deserve any treasure! Miserable louts. I'll mark this place. Come back later.*

Cursing under his breath, Pierre tucked the coin in his pocket and placed the figure back in the box. He covered the old container with bark and leaves. *Almost like a bed.* He bent down and sat on a smooth black rock. *Tired. Want to lie down here and sleep. This is different. Aching in head and stomach. Damn foreman.* Pierre coughed, and his lunch erupted from his stomach.

He kicked his foot out, hitting the end of the box. An ancient helmet dislodged from under a shrub. It rolled past his boot, exposing crumbling yellowish matter, some teeth, and a bee's nest. Pierre jumped to his feet and inhaled a lungful of the damp jungle air. He slipped on his vomit and grasped a nearby vine to steady himself. *Ow! A ghost guards this gold! No wonder I feel lousy! Evil spirits are here.*

Pierre took the small ax from the sheath at his waist and walked to a tall Giant Kapok tree. He hacked three diagonal marks in the bark as he stumbled unsteadily in the direction of the foreman's whistles. As Pierre lurched forward, he lost control of his bowels and threw up again. He took his canteen from his web belt and cleaned his mouth as best he could. *Must rest.*

A brown, triangular head on a sturdy, patterned body rose from the dark leaves at the base of a tree, recoiled, and struck Pierre's thigh. "Yeow!" He shrieked in pain and fear, slashing as the snake's fangs stuck in the thin cotton of his filthy pantaloons. Pierre grabbed the writhing serpent and threw it into the foliage—but not until the fangs had stabbed his hand, lacerated and swollen from the day's work and the ants.

Disoriented from the attack, Pierre rose and staggered in circles shouting for help. He held his aching head. His thigh and hand were pulsating with fire. He followed the sound of voices to the other workers. Pierre screamed in agony as the toxin coursed through his body. He bent and vomited again, nausea overwhelming him.

Maurice grabbed him and examined Pierre's wounds and tattered, soiled clothing. "It was probably a Fer-de-Lance, Pierre," Maurice said as he and another team member laid him down in the wet grass. Shaking their heads at one another in dismay, Maurice ventured, "I never heard of a bite taking hold so quick." He grabbed his water bag and dampened a rag. He put it on Pierre's forehead and watched helplessly as Pierre writhed, the poison coursing through his body. The smell of emptying bowels caused the men to back away. Pierre became still, paralysis overtaking his muscles. His eyes clouded over; they no longer saw the sky, the jungle, or the men around him.

They buried Pierre next to the trail he helped survey. No one thought to look in the pockets of his soiled pantaloons.

PART I
JANUARY 2018

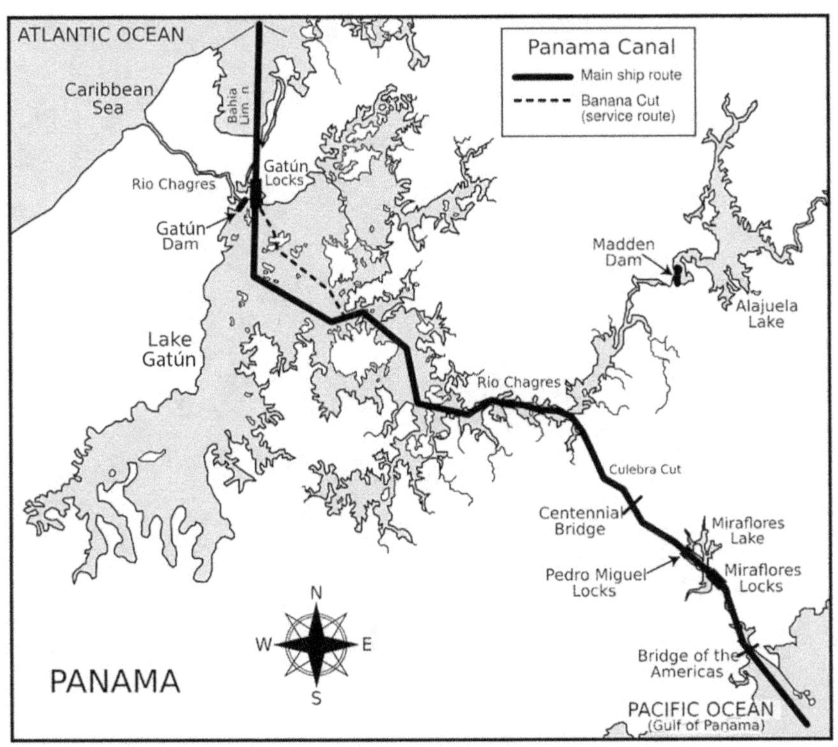

LANNY MITCHELL

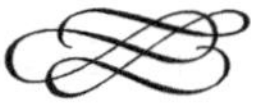

Infinite shades of green—both exciting and calming. So different from Albuquerque. God, I love this country. This is the haven I need now. Lanny's mind was racing as the Boeing 737 descended toward Panama City and the Pacific Ocean. She saw her grin reflected in the window of the plane and couldn't resist the urge to laugh. *Time to recover and enjoy all this place's got to offer.*

She turned from the lowering sun through her window to the ashen woman in the next seat, smiled sympathetically, and said, "All's well. Here we are, safe and sound on the ground! I'll bet our pilot was with the Air Force. He greased it on the runway. A great omen for your trip, and mine, too."

Lanny exited the security area after getting her wheeled duffle and spotted a familiar figure. "Alejandro!" She gave the youngish Panamanian in the crumpled white linen suit a great bear hug.

Responding to the hug with a smile, Alejandro Galvez took off his hat and bowed. "*Señorita* Lanny, *Buenas tardes.* Welcome back. How was your trip?"

"Very good up to this point. This bag and my backpack are all I've got, so we're ready to go."

Alejandro said, "We will find more beautiful and interesting birds for you. I talked with the other guides. We have current information on where to go. Are you ready?"

"Yes, let's go."

"Let me take the bag for you. *Señorita* Lanny, did you get my birthday card?"

"I did, Alejandro. Thanks for remembering. It was a memorable forty." They both laughed. *If he noticed my laugh was stressed, he didn't show it. It's so much easier if I don't have to make explanations.*

Alejandro led their way through the Tocumen International Airport open-air parking lot to an extremely dirty brown Land Rover. He paid to exit the lot and enter the highway, and Lanny leaned back in her seat, gazing at the greenery going by. She listened to Alejandro's gentle voice, making plans for her days, nodded off, and was surprised to wake up to him saying, "*Señorita* Lanny. We are here." With a flourish, the young man continued, "This is *Finca Paraíso*—an old family estate with a very new boutique hotel."

A distinguished-looking gentleman approached them as they exited the Land Rover. Alejandro spoke over the bag in his arms, "*Señorita* Pamela Mitchell, may I present *Señor* Jorge Sanchez de Piños. Welcome to his hotel."

"*Buenas noches, Señor* Sanchez," Lanny said, proffering a hand to the black-haired, slender gentleman approaching them. "And please call me Lanny."

Jorge's thick dark eyebrows framed deep brown eyes surrounded by cavernous lines emphasizing his broad smile. Instead of shaking her hand, Jorge took it, bent, and kissed it. His dense salt and pepper mustache tickled where it touched her fingers. Jorge's sparkling eyes drew an involuntary smile from Lanny.

"*Buena noches, Señorita.* This is an old custom, but then, I am old-fashioned when it comes to lovely ladies," Jorge said.

A tremor jostled both before he released her hand. Lanny's eyes widened, and she gave a nervous chuckle. "That was startling! *Señor,* I don't normally feel the earth shake when someone kisses my hand. You must have a direct line to the heavens."

"This was a first, but I will work on it."

Alejandro turned to Lanny. "*Señor* Sanchez is my uncle, my godfather, and my mentor. When my parents died, he took me under his wing." He grinned and added, "I have him to thank for my education at the Cornell Lab of Ornithology."

"So, this is the guardian angel you've told me about."

"*Sí, Señorita* Lanny."

Jorge beamed and told Lanny, "Dinner is over, but perhaps you will join me in my private dining room for a late supper?"

"I'm not dressed as elegantly as you. The flight was long, and I haven't changed clothes since leaving Miami." Lanny felt her stomach growl, "On the other hand, I'm famished. Thank you, I'd love to join you. Alejandro, are you coming as well?"

"No, *Señorita* Lanny, I will put my gear in my room and go visit my friend. Miguel is also a guide and will share information we can use tomorrow. He was birding the area today with a group. His wife is a wonderful cook, so I too will be well fed."

JORGE SANCHEZ

Lanny and Jorge were seated at a table near the edge of an outdoor portal where the trickling sound of an indoor waterfall was background music for their conversation. An overhead palm fan whirred, slowly pushing around the hot, humid air.

"Please, tell me about this lovely place. I only got a glimpse before it was too dark to see anything," Lanny said after they had touched the rims of their wine glasses. She sipped a cool chardonnay and remarked, "This is excellent. French?"

"No, *Señorita* Mitchell, I opened a bottle of Chalone in your honor."

"Please, call me Lanny. Really." Her tongue licked her lips as she tasted the buttery wine and recalled visiting the Chalone vineyards near Pinnacles National Park in California, celebrating after her first view of California Condors.

"All right, Lanny, it is. Then you must call me Jorge."

They appraised each other, then Lanny looked down at her glass. *He's charming, how old? Sort of timeless…do I care? Just recuperating here.*

"Did you notice the view as you came onto the property?"

"No, Jorge, I'm afraid I nodded off on the drive."

"You will get to appreciate the view in the morning. But in the meantime, this estate is on the side of a sleeping volcano. Our main crop is coffee. You will enjoy some with your breakfast."

"Wonderful. Thank you for realizing that hot coffee—the caffeine—and the excitement of being here would keep me awake tonight in spite of my fatigue. Tomorrow, I will appreciate it."

"Of course. We grow our coffee under tall trees, so it is rich and flavorful. The trees protect the coffee plants."

Lanny leaned back, "I make it a point at home to buy shade-grown coffee. The trees give birds habitat."

"True. Both trees and plants attract birds, and birders, like you, follow, filling our rooms with visitors."

Jorge continued throughout dinner, telling Lanny about the area and *Volcán de Oro*. He explained the dormant volcano named for an old gold mine provided the lush setting for his boutique hotel. And the small coffee crop provided some extra income to pay for the more than ample staff at the hotel.

After dinner, Jorge showed Lanny to her room. "Now that it would not disturb our dinner, I would like to express my sorrow for the loss of your friend. Since Mr. Preston was to be here also, Alejandro has shared all his information with me, so I can understand if you seem unhappy. Please know that you can have privacy or share as you wish. It is not the same, but since my wife has died, I am more, um…um…aware of heart issues than before. I am at your service if I can be helpful."

Her eyes filled with tears; Lanny's lips trembled as she tried to gain control of her emotions. "*Señor* Jorge, thank you for your kindness. It helps more than you know."

Jorge bowed very slightly and turned toward the path to his house at the rear of the property. "Ah, then I will bid you *buenas noches,* Miss Lanny."

She sniffled and found a tissue in her pocket. *Damn. That was sweet but brought all the feelings to the surface again.* She lingered on the covered walkway, enjoying the subtle lighting in the trees and shrubs, listening to the sounds of insects in the woods. *Loud cicadas. Crickets. Are those bumblebees? At night?* She realized her fatigue with a smothered yawn. And then the ground shook again. *OMG, is Ms. Volcán de Oro angry? A Latin version of Hawaii's Pele?*

MORNING WITH ALEJANDRO GALVEZ

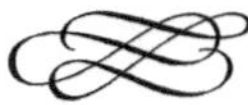

A nearby owl called, the loud screech bringing Lanny instantly out of bed and to her feet in near-complete darkness. *Barn Owl? What?* Disoriented, she pivoted, getting her bearings. "Did I miss my alarm? What time is it? Where…?" Finding her phone, she relaxed. *Ten minutes till the alarm. OK, so a familiar call. I'm awake.* Lanny downed a protein bar for a quick breakfast while dressing. *Coffee will wait 'til later.*

When Alejandro drove up in his Land Rover, she was ready—his cheery nature reflected in his broad smile. Even at this early hour, his eyes gleamed with joy. His khaki shirt and pants didn't hide the sturdy muscles developed from carrying bags and equipment for all his clients. He tossed her backpack in the vehicle as if it were a feather.

"As usual, *Señorita* Lanny, you are quick to go. Our arrival in the evening did not let you appreciate how beautiful this area is, but we will cover much of it in our time here. *Volcán de Oro* is beautiful. Today we stay at the base since we are starting late."

"A late start? A few minutes after six? I forgot what you think is early...." Lanny laughed as she climbed into the vehicle. "I'm amazed you are still relying on this antique Land Rover."

"*Sí, Señorita.* 1989 was an excellent year for these four-wheel drives. Maybe it was a good year for Panama also."

Lanny held her reaction as she realized he was talking about the U.S. invasion in 1989 and the Noriega regime's end.

Alejandro snapped his fingers. "I have a special surprise for you. My friend Miguel found a new Army Ant bivouac. We'll go tomorrow—all the antbirds will be there."

"Wonderful. Those birds will be lifers for my list. What a treat! You know this is a new part of the country for me. Right next to the canal. I'm excited. Too bad there isn't a way to fly low and slow over it in my hang glider. I guess hiking through it, and glimpses from the volcano will do instead."

They walked trails in the vicinity of the estate for the rest of the day, working to find a Turaco and others which had eluded her on previous trips. Even in lightweight clothing, Lanny was still not conditioned to the heat of the tropics. Stopping to wipe her brow and feeling another tremor, she asked, "Alejandro, anything to worry about with the volcano?"

"No, *Volcán de Oro* is known for sometimes letting us know she is not dead. But she has not erupted in many centuries."

CHEN ZHOU

陈舟

Lanny was tired after a full day of birding. Her stomach growled during a quick shower, reminding her she needed food, although sleep sounded even better. The hairdryer made quick work of her new, short haircut. Delighted with the ease of styling, she flipped her head from side to side to make it swing. *Yes indeed, just what I needed. Wash and wear!*

The cheerful dining room at the hotel revived her. Lanny sat at the only empty table, idly listening to the hum of voices, and enjoying the breeze carrying the aromas of flowers and the sounds of bees pollinating them. A voice at her elbow interrupted her daydreaming.

"Miss, would you mind if I joined you?"

She glanced up to discover a well-dressed, solid-looking Asian gentleman, with a shock of straight salt and pepper hair, standing beside the empty chair at her table. His open expression included a tentative smile exposing a gold bicuspid. He stood as if poised to retreat while he waited for her answer.

"Please," Lanny said, returning his smile. She waved her hand at the empty seat, "I prefer not eating alone. Are you staying here at the *finca*?" She wondered how precise his English was and how much she needed to simplify her language or slow down her speech to be understood.

Sitting, he replied, "Indeed, yes. May I introduce myself? My name is Chen Zhou."

He reached into his sports jacket pocket and extracted a card. "I'm the representative of a Chinese investment company here in Panama and want to do some birding on my few days' vacation."

Smiling, Lanny said, "My name is Lanny Mitchell. I'm here for the same reason. Birding is my relatively new hobby, and Panama's got so many birds, it's exciting to be here."

"Yes, this area is renowned for a large variety of species, and I too wish to add to my life list, but I find it challenging to distinguish birds in this heavy foliage,"

"I agree with you. Spotting birds in these dense woods isn't easy." She read the card and asked, "What sort of ventures is your company working on?"

Chen Zhou　陈舟

Chinese-Panamanian Ventures 中巴风险投资
Empresas chino-panameñas
Avenida Samuel Lewis, Torre ADR, Pisa 13,
Ciudad de Panamá, Panamá
+507 380-2345

"China has multiple trade agreements with Panama. My specialty is transportation. And you, what is your occupation?"

"I'm a recovering lawyer from Albuquerque, New Mexico. I had a career in environmental issues, usually after a disaster."

"Recovering lawyer?"

"Sorry, I mean to say that I've given up my practice." Her mouth tensed, and she looked again at the card as a distraction.

Zhou squinted and tilted his head to one side.

Lanny put the card to the side of her plate. As she heard Zhou speak, she realized his English was nearly equivalent to a native-born American speaker. "Here's the waiter. I'm starving."

BIRDS OF A FEATHER

They ordered chicken *sancocho*, a hearty stew-like soup, and Lanny added extra *yuca frita*. She asked Zhou, "You tried these local fries?" When he shook his head, she explained, "Yuca is a favorite of mine. It's kind of like a potato but with half the carbs. I'll be glad to share it."

"I would enjoy the new experience. Miss Mitchell, are you on holiday? You said you too were looking for birds."

"Yes, Mr. Zhou."

"Excuse me, but my first name is Zhou, and my family name is Chen. You pronounce Zhou like Joe in English."

"Sorry, I didn't realize."

"No harm. It's a common mistake."

"To answer your question, I've come to Panama before on short birding tours through International Avian Adventures. This time I'm again independently hiring a guide. This way, we can adapt our plans to chase target birds to add to my life list."

"What a great opportunity. How many birds are on your life list?"

"Well, so far, only about 3,000. I got a late start, but lately, I have been concentrating on it."

"Very good. I have a little over 6,500. Remember, China is a vast country with many different environments and, therefore, many different birds. Also, traveling for my company gave me other opportunities."

"Really, how long've you been birding?"

They talked throughout the meal. Everything from numbers of birds per year to most unusual birds seen, comfortable clothing, best binoculars, and whether the latest iPhone took clear enough photos for their records.

Lanny explained she had hired Alejandro, the guide from earlier trips who had become a friend. "This part of Panama is new to me, so having Alejandro, who knows the area and the birds, is helpful. I plan an extended stay and am even considering moving to live here full time."

"Excellent. There are many benefits for ex-patriots who sign up for the *Turista Pensionado* program."

"Yes, I'm aware of that and brought all the necessary documentation with me to apply."

Lanny discovered why Zhou's command of the language was so good. He'd gone to school at the University of Southern California and had worked hard to become fluent in American English.

"I have been here for a few days birding by myself," Zhou said. "I got somewhat lost on the trails near the estate. I am concerned about walking further without a local guide," His furrowed brow creasing his oval face reflected his worry.

"The density of tropical forests makes it hard to find trails, and spotting the birds is difficult. It takes patience and luck, or an experienced guide," Lanny agreed.

She smiled warmly at Zhou and offered, "I'm sure Alejandro, my guide for this trip, will not object to having another birding enthusiast along. Would you like to join us tomorrow? We are going along the base of the *Volcán de Oro*. A friend of Alejandro's found an Army Ant bivouac, and that means..."

"Antbirds!" Zhou exclaimed before Lanny could finish her explanation. His face lit up with delight. "I know about them from reading and hoped to find them, but they are, what is the word, 'skulky,' only trailing the ants, hiding under plants."

"That's an accurate description. The way they make their living is fascinating—using ants to find their food. Different species adapted to catching various bugs the ants scare up and miss. Not that the ants are trying to help, they are after their own meals."

"Miss Mitchell, if you are sure it will not be an imposition, I would like to join you tomorrow."

Zhou inclined his head as she said: "Please call me Lanny. Joining us won't be an imposition. I wouldn't have offered if I weren't serious. A warning, however, we'll leave quite early. You will also need to make arrangements with Alejandro for his fee. We'll meet at the front door, ready to go, at five in the morning. Does that make you change your mind?"

Zhou laughed and responded, flashing his gold bicuspid, "Not at all; I'm usually an early riser. And please call me Zhou. I'll leave you now so I can get some sleep. Again, thank you for your company."

VOLCÁN DE ORO

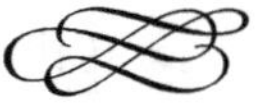

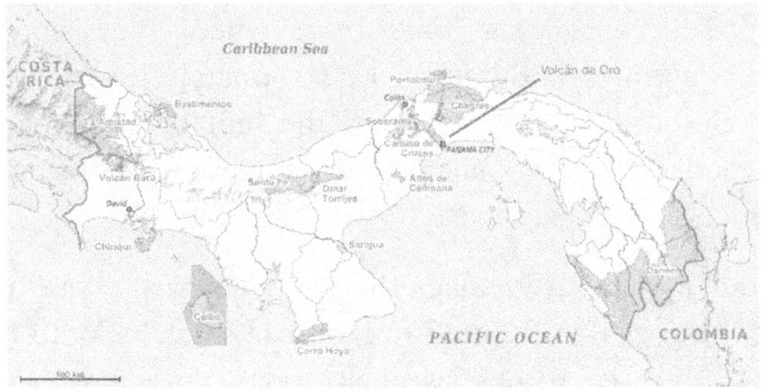

I t was still dark at fifteen minutes before five in the morning when Lanny got to the hotel's front and found Alejandro parked in the drive.

"*Buenas días*, Alejandro. How're you this morning?"

"Very good, *Señorita* Lanny. You are prompt, as usual. Are you ready to leave?"

"Well, not quite. I took the liberty of inviting another birder to join us. I was sure you wouldn't mind. However, I told him what time to meet us, and if he isn't here soon, we will go on. His name is Chen Zhou."

Alejandro asked, "Zhou is his first name?"

"Yes, he was trying to find birds without a helpful guide like you." They both turned as they heard footsteps. "Here he is, a little early as well. Good morning, Zhou. This is Alejandro."

"Alejandro, a pleasure." Beaming at them, Zhou said, "I understand Lanny hired you for several days, and I would like to join you today."

The two men shook hands, finished introductions, and settled their business arrangement. Alejandro loaded their belongings into the Land Rover, and they departed to find the Army Ants. Before sunrise at six o'clock, they followed an old dirt road near some railroad tracks. After a few minutes, they took a turn on a dirt road that circled the *Volcán de Oro's* base, where they stopped and unloaded equipment and backpacks. Fortunately, it was cool as they traversed the jungle. They followed the hint of a footpath into a heavily wooded, shallow valley, winding toward the rising slope of the volcano.

"Keep your eyes open for flags that will show us where my friend Miguel left the trail and found the ants. He was lucky to find their bivouac so that we can observe them today," Alejandro told Zhou. Several yards back, Lanny had stopped to observe a Glass-winged Butterfly whose erratic flight intrigued her.

She caught up to Alejandro and Zhou in time to hear Alejandro add, "The ants stay in one spot for several days, and foraging parties go out each day to catch insects and spiders. They bring their kill back to the bivouac to share with the queen and the workers."

Alejandro pointed to an orange flag on a wire stake. "Here is Miguel's marker. Watch where you step. We should be early enough; the ants are still waking up, but…" Alejandro's voice trailed off as he led them farther into the dense thickets crowding the valley.

"*¡Mira!*–look. Here is the bivouac. The ants are beginning to move out from their sleeping place." Alejandro gestured toward a dark mass draping over a fallen log and on an intersecting leaning branch. "*Mira*, the ants are passing that way. The lead foragers have already started, and others are beginning to follow."

Pointing, he added, "We can go ahead of them and watch the birds come as the ants miss some of the insects." Paralleling the moving stream, the three hurried to get just ahead of the scurrying mass, staying yards away from the increasing parade.

"*Mira*, there is a Dot-winged Antwren, and next to it, Chestnut-backed Antbird. Over to the right of the low palm, a Checker-throated Antwren." Alejandro started calling out the names of birds faster than Lanny and Zhou could follow. They were dazzled by the number and variety of antbirds. Activity filled the undergrowth, and all three were pointing and exclaiming over the different species they were watching.

A smiling Zhou wiped his brow with a white handkerchief and used it to swat away some bees. He then told Alejandro he wanted to get far ahead of the ants to watch the interaction between insects and birds and take a photo. The ant swarm forged ahead, and the two men followed, stumbling on loose rocks and rotten tree limbs.

Lanny stopped to peer at some unusual rocks and a slight crack in the ground. Wisps of steam rose from the fissure. She bent over and let her binoculars fall to the end of their strap. She shook her head and stood. *What a terrible headache. Ugh, I'm nauseated. Ooh, I guess it's the excitement.*

Zhou and Alejandro were some distance ahead in the jungle, almost out of sight. They were excited, spotting still more species. For a moment, Lanny was ignored. She took a deep breath before trying to stand erect without vomiting and was stunned to observe several birds down the gentle slope lying on their backs on the ground near her. One was feebly flapping a wing, another's legs were twitching, but several more—different species—were totally still.

"Alejandro! Please! Come back! I need some help here."

DEAD ANTBIRDS

Alejandro spun around and ran to her.

Lanny had a hand on a tree to support herself and stared at the dead birds at her feet. She looked up as the anxious guide stopped in front of her. "I feel awful." She grimaced. "I'm nauseated and woozy."

"*Señorita* Lanny! What is the matter?"

"I don't know. I suddenly felt ill, sick to my stomach. Let me just sit and rest for a while."

Lanny sat on a rock and slowly began to recover her wits. Alejandro offered her some water, but she didn't want anything. After a few minutes, she said, "Check under the edge of the bushes. There are several birds dead or dying!"

"*Señorita* Lanny! Stand up! Lean on me instead—before that Bullet Ant finds you." Alejandro put his arm around her waist to keep her from falling as her legs suddenly gave way. He stared at her with wide eyes. "You need help. We must get you back to the hotel fast and call for a doctor."

Lanny felt better as he helped her away from the spot where she had fallen ill. "Alejandro, this is a nuisance. I was fine until just a few minutes ago—this horrible headache. And my eyes are playing tricks. I'm sure it will pass."

Zhou tripped and fell while returning through the foliage. He picked himself up and hurried to them. "What is the problem? Lanny is ill?"

Alejandro explained the situation and that they were going back to the *finca* as fast as possible. He pointed out the curious situation of the dead and dying birds.

Zhou offered, "Lanny, I can hold your backpack. Do you want some water?"

Lanny gave him a weak smile. "Thanks, I'll let you take the backpack. No water now, though."

"Lanny and Alejandro, I will stay here a minute and try to understand what happened to these birds." Zhou looked at the birds on the ground, and he said to Alejandro, "You brought some plastic bags, right?"

"*Sí, Señor* Chen."

"Then I suggest we gather up some of these birds and take them back with us. Lanny, can you wait a minute before we get you back to the Land Rover? I will record this location on my phone."

Lanny simply nodded and concentrated on breathing carefully.

Before filling bags, Zhou pulled his smartphone from his pocket and tapped the screen. He tapped some more and took a video, aiming the device at the forest, pivoting to capture its appearance. He then focused on the birds, all of which Lanny noted were now still.

Alejandro grabbed a couple of small clear plastic bags from his backpack and gave them to Zhou. He put one over his hand as a glove and quickly picked up half a dozen birds as he walked into the brush.

Zhou walked toward the other two and bent over to pick up something. He put it and his phone in his pocket. "Alejandro, please bag some of this soil as well."

"*Sí, Señor* Chen." Alejandro bagged some soil and returned. "There are more dead birds beyond this vine tangle, but I think we need to get *Señorita* Lanny back."

QUESTIONS

Zhou carried her backpack, and with the two of them helping, sometimes almost carrying Lanny, they got to the Land Rover without incident.

After they were several miles along the unpaved road, Lanny spoke up from the back seat. "Ugh! That was scary, but my headache and stomach are much better. Now I want to know what's going on."

She shook her head, grimaced, and went on. "Resting back here… I've been thinking. I lingered in one area for a while when you two kept hiking ahead. And maybe, whatever affected me also killed the birds? They were ground birds with tiny bodies. What could be killing them? Some plant? What? The ants weren't bothering them."

Alejandro shrugged his shoulders, "I do not know, *Señorita* Lanny. I have never seen anything like this in all my years as a guide."

Zhou turned to Lanny and said, "I am hopeful we can find some answers."

Alejandro snapped his fingers. "Perhaps my friend Bernardo in the biology lab at the *Universidad de Panamá* has seen this before."

Zhou turned to Alejandro. "Excellent suggestion. Talking to a professional is a good idea. Can you do that today?"

"*Sí, Señor* Chen. I will take these birds and the soil samples to him, and we will find out what he says."

They rode in silence the rest of the way to the hotel, where Lanny insisted she was well enough to avoid the effort of finding a doctor. She asked to look at the birds before Alejandro departed. Not opening the plastic bags, Alejandro laid them on the bench at the entry and gently moved the little bodies, separating them from one another.

"They are definitely all ground birds, aren't they, Alejandro? Maybe, at most, they'd get a foot or two off it, on a branch?"

"That is so, *Señorita* Lanny. These Antbirds stay close to the ground, some even nesting just inches up in small shrubs. I wonder, though, if something killed them, why didn't it affect the ants?"

"Good question. Perhaps your biologist friend, what's his name again, can give us more information. When you two talk, I'd like to meet him."

Alejandro answered, "His name is Doctor Bernardo Cruz; he's a professor in the university's biology department."

Zhou added, "And please allow me to attend as well."

Lanny raised an eyebrow and said, "Of course. You marked the location on your phone, you've got the video, and you were there with us. Meanwhile, I'm going to take a nap and try to get rid of this headache. I still don't feel completely like myself, but can we meet again as planned, after *siesta*?"

Alejandro said, "Whatever you say, *Señorita* Lanny. Perhaps Mr. Chen can forward the location and the video to my phone. It will help with my explaining to Bernardo."

Zhou inclined his head and said, "Of course."

Lanny smiled at Alejandro and turned to Zhou. "That's a great idea. I'm not intending to fall over again and need a pack carrier, but your ideas will be a welcome addition. Three o'clock, here, gentlemen?"

Zhou and Alejandro handled the transfer of the GPS coordinates and the video.

"In the meantime, I will carry these specimen bags and the digital files to my friend Doctor Bernardo." Alejandro picked up the specimens, hugged Lanny, and left.

Zhou and Lanny watched the Land Rover depart, and Lanny glanced at her watch. "It feels like a full day already, but it's not even nine o'clock. I'm going to lie down and hope to feel even better soon," Lanny said.

"So, you are not recovered then?"

"No, not completely. I think I just need to lie down."

"The dining room is still open, would breakfast help you?" Zhou inquired.

"Thanks, but food doesn't sound like the right thing now. I simply want to be alone in my room for a while."

"Miss Mitchell, the occurrence this morning was quite strange—a little frightening. I would like to know what caused the death of those birds and your reaction."

PART II
CONUNDRUM

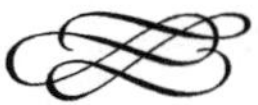

DOCTOR BERNARDO CRUZ

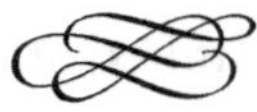

Alejandro was standing by his Land Rover at the curb when Lanny appeared.

"Amazing! A short rest, a cool washcloth, a quiet room, and a light lunch with your uncle Jorge, and I'm repaired. And here is Zhou, on time." She smiled at both men, waiting until they finished greetings.

Alejandro held the Land Rover door open for Lanny. Zhou helped himself into the back seat.

"Alejandro, did you obtain any information for us about the birds?"

"*Sí, Señor* Chen, but let me get us on the road first."

Instead of heading in the direction they took in the morning, Alejandro turned toward Panamá as the locals referred to Panama City. "My friend Bernardo was in his office this morning. He is interested in our birds and will ask the main lab at the *Universidad* to do necropsies. But that will be later and take some time. He wants to show us the video and hear from you what happened to you, *Señorita* Lanny."

Lanny turned to the rear seat, "Zhou, did you bring your phone? If we lose definition when it's enlarged, your phone might be handy."

"Of course, Lanny. I never go anywhere without it." Zhou held up his latest model iPhone.

"I should have guessed. We probably won't need it. Did you watch the video? Were you able to uncover anything new?" Lanny asked.

"I watched it, but details are limited at phone size. It will be better if it's larger."

"*Señor* Chen, there is new equipment in Bernardo's lab. There will be a big-screen display for the video."

Doctor Bernardo Cruz was not the older, staid, fusty, academic ornithologist, busy with birdlife details, Lanny had expected. *No rings on fingers. Good. Great hair, gorgeous eyes. Disarming smile and whoo, smokin' hot body. Can't help but wonder...* surprised at her reaction, she stopped that train of thought and squelched a guilty smile as Bernardo addressed her.

"*Buenas tardes, Señorita* Mitchell," Bernardo said with a firm but not an overwhelming handshake. He turned to Zhou and Alejandro, giving Lanny a moment to control the sizzling impulse that ran up her arm from his touch.

"Alejandro told me about your adventure this morning—that is not the right word. Your unpleasant experience. I want to know more about where you were and how long you had been there, but first, I think we should watch the video."

Bernardo led them to his computer, its large screen glowing, just waiting for them to sit in the lab chairs he pulled into viewing range as he talked. He called up the file and displayed it.

"OK, here is the forest and the scan of the area, but when Zhou concentrates on the ground with the birds' bodies, look at this dark shape under the edge of the farther bush. Follow this arrow." Bernardo drew a line around a dim shape.

Lanny was the first to speak. "Is that? …that looks like a bucket, no, a helmet. What kind of helmet would be in the jungle?"

Bernardo beamed at Lanny—the smile of a teacher to a favorite student or a pet who has done a perfect trick. Momentarily dazzled, she pulled herself back to what he was saying. "Excellent observation. I think a helmet too. Zhou, can you show me on a map exactly where you recorded this?"

Zhou extracted his iPhone and showed Bernardo the location he noted on his app. Bernardo unfolded a topographical map of the *Parque nacional Camino de Cruces* and the *Parque nacional Soberanía* areas. Alejandro pointed out where they hiked, and they used Zhou's information for more precision.

Bernardo stroked his chin. "We should consider who was near an old volcano and wore a helmet like this. The canal runs close to where you were, but the men who worked on construction in the late 1800s and early 1900s were not wearing anything like these helmets."

Lanny spoke up again, "So if it is older than the beginning of the American canal or even the French, then what are the logical possibilities? The Spanish had a lengthy history of exploration here. The pirate Henry Morgan sacked *Panamá la Vieja* and looted the gold." She fumbled with her phone and wished she were at her laptop, where Google quickly had all the answers, and she could take advantage of the larger screen.

Zhou cleared his throat and spoke. "When I knew I was going to be in Panama as part of my job, I studied the country's history. Spanish explorer Balboa was the first European to cross the isthmus, but the French were the first to attempt to create a canal."

Bernardo nodded. "You are right. The French were first, but the combination of inadequate engineering expertise and rampant illnesses stopped them. The ditch waited until the U.S. took over in 1904. But none of those men wore helmets like this. I think *Señorita* Mitchell is correct. Those earlier Spanish *conquistadores* wore *morions,* helmets in English, with the flared edge. Easy to mistake them for a bucket. Now I want you to look at this."

REMEMBER THE BIRDS

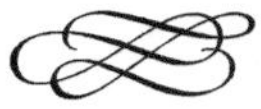

Deciding the *conquistadores'* details could wait, Lanny darkened her screen to concentrate on Bernardo's request.

He returned to the beginning of the video and then stopped it on the landscape. Enlarging a part of it, he took a screenshot so they could view it without any confusion.

"What do you think this is? I am ready for ideas since I have none." Bernardo gave a self-deprecating laugh.

Lanny leaned forward to peer at the grainy picture. Poking up from the soil was a tent-shaped, triangular object. "I'm betting manufactured. If I were a fan of sci-fi, I'd say it was a pyramid for tiny aliens." Shrugging her shoulders, she sat back to think about it from a different angle. *Stop volunteering. Just an opportunity to be wrong. Enough of that. Hey, self, get over it…you promised no more.*

"What do you think, *Señor* Chen?" Bernardo asked.

Zhou's face was a mass of crinkles and furrows as he considered the item in the photo. "It appears old. Stained as it is with dirt and plant growth, it did not get there yesterday." Zhou tilted his head and leaned closer to the screen. "Could it be the cap on something? It is a strange shape for any container."

Bernardo looked quizzically at Alejandro, who shrugged his shoulders, "*No sé*. I have never seen anything like this."

"Maybe it's related to whatever made me sick. I'm ready to go back and find out! I like having answers to things, and I sure didn't like the way something got to me." Lanny slapped her leg repeatedly.

"Are you sure you are up to returning? That 'something' is still there." Zhou looked at the screen, avoiding Lanny's stare. *Tired of not being in control. Unhappy with assumptions made. Tired, too, of being second-guessed.*

She hesitated and regarded her audience. "Don't look at me like I'm some delicate flower. Returning is important. I can protect myself this time. There's something unhealthy going on, and I want to know what. It wasn't just me affected by it. We are sidetracked by artifacts; remember the birds."

No one said anything for a minute. Zhou continued to scrutinize the monitor with the photo still in place. Alejandro regarded Bernardo, expecting him to say something.

Arrgh! If I sit here any longer…. It's like work was! Men who thought they knew it all. Irritated, Lanny stood and slipped between Zhou and Alejandro to get away from the computer and into the more spacious part of the lab. Crossing her arms over her chest, she paced the length of the room. *Dammit. They don't want to make a commitment to go back. So, what now? I need support, not fearful protection. Don't they want to know what is there too?*

She turned after looking at labels on cabinets. Hearing Bernardo's voice, she lengthened her stride and got close enough to listen to him, saying, "…yes, bird populations are affected by many things. It could have been that the insects they prey on ate something toxic, or perhaps they were affected by chemicals in the water they drank. I will not know until the technicians return their analysis."

Lanny remained standing, arms still crossed. Her stiff posture reflected her feelings. *What are they thinking? A simple answer? Too dangerous to risk going back. Forget that. They aren't trained to think about environmental problems.* She clipped her response. "Thanks for sharing the video. I didn't spend much time dilly-dallying around after I felt ill, but I'll look more carefully when I get back there, and I intend to bring back those two mysterious objects. Please let me know when you hear something about the birds or the soil samples."

She started moving toward the door, and the three men rose as one. Zhou dropped his phone under one of the tables and retrieved it. After a round of handshaking, Alejandro led them back to the Land Rover.

Zhou got in the back seat, leaving Lanny to sulk in front. Her rigid back and tightly gripped hands said more than words about her displeasure at minimizing the reason for the birds dying.

Zhou spoke up. "Lanny, perhaps there's more we can do. Perhaps we can find a private firm in Panamá that could analyze my video and the birds…"

Alejandro replied before Lanny could speak. "*Señor* Chen, I'm afraid Panama is not like China in scale. If my friend cannot get satisfaction from the main lab, I will ask him if he can send the bodies on ice and the soil samples to the U.S. If not, then I think we should just forget the whole thing."

Lanny gave Alejandro a quick look, then stared ahead in silence for the rest of the ride to the *finca*. *Guess these guys weren't brought up on activism. After fighting every step to be considered or included, it feels right to do it again.*

A HOLE IN THE ESCUDO

Zhou crossed the dining room to the table where Lanny was finishing her meal. "May I join you?"

"Please do. I'm going in circles thinking about this problem. I'm sure there is something dangerous going on." Lanny took a sip of coffee.

"None of us are scientists, but what we experienced was not normal. And your sudden illness was bizarre."

Lanny nodded, "And I didn't touch anything, so I am thinking whatever affected me had to be in the air. The internet's got lots of information on volcanos. We were on one that is 'dormant.' It seems some volcanos are sources of mercury vapor. Maybe in that steam we saw. I had all of the symptoms of mercury vapor poisoning listed on MedicineNet."

Zhou spoke up again. "This is a new issue. We need to investigate it. Did you notice the wind while we were there? Is the problem from somewhere else? We can wear a mask of some kind. We should wear gloves."

Her eyebrows rose as she peered over her cup. This was a new side of Zhou. "This *Volcán de Oro* is rocking and rolling now. Tremors for the last several weeks, according to one of the waiters. I've felt several myself."

"Lanny, are you sure you want to go back where we were this morning? It is hard to absorb that it was only this morning that you were sickened. I want to know about the object we saw in the video. That poor look at the darkness under bushes was not enough. Maybe it is valuable. Perhaps the helmet is just a beginning."

Lanny stood. "I'm ready to go to the volcano again. I agree we need some protection. Whether or not it's mercury fumes, something is causing sickness. Alejandro is expecting us at six o'clock in the morning, so we can go birding away from the ant location until stores open, and we find protective masks."

Zhou rose.

Lanny yawned, "I'm heading for my room and rest. Catch you in the morning?"

"This is more exciting than I planned, but I am pleased to be included. Maybe I can be of help," Zhou said. "I will be there at six o'clock. Wishing you a refreshing sleep." With that, he bowed, turned on his heel, and departed.

Zhou looked in the mirror and curled his lip as he finished flossing around his gold bicuspid. *Time now to do some research. One more look at it.* He carried his toiletries kit to the bed, turned it upside down, and dumped the contents on the coverlet. Righting the container, he lifted a corner of the lining and pried up the cardboard underneath. He tapped the end of the case in his hand and caught the shiny coin as it fell out. He had picked it up on *Volcán de Oro* before he rejoined Alejandro and Lanny.

Zhou carried the coin to the small desk and used his reading magnifier and a small flashlight to get a clearer view. *The worn number is 1670. Must be a date. Over three hundred years old.* Zhou thought to himself as he rolled the crude gold coin in his palm: *Why this off-center hole? For a necklace?*

Zhou opened his MacBook Pro and logged on to the hotel's Wi-Fi network. He was rewarded with pictures of several coins that might have come from the same cache. *A Spanish gold escudo. Maybe even minted in Bolivia. Each worth over 9,000 American dollars!*

Zhou leaned back in his desk chair, closed his eyes, and contemplated the ceiling. *Panamá was a passage for South American gold going to Spain. Except when it didn't make it. Where there's one, maybe...*

Thinking about Miss Mitchell, he raised the corner of his upper lip as he was drifting off to sleep. Her perky breasts, turquoise-blue eyes, a tinge of gray in her auburn hair, and her simple swingy-cut bob hairdo. So unlike the local women or those back home. His last thoughts were to collect some soil for his compatriots when they were near the mountain tomorrow.

NEAR-MISS

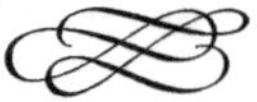

Six o'clock in the morning found both Lanny and Zhou greeting Alejandro at the curb.

"*Señorita* Lanny, we have options on places to go today. The area near our first day's visit has more habitats to explore, or…"

Lanny spoke up before he could go on. "Please. I would like to do some birding near the highway so we can buy gas masks as soon as a store opens. Zhou and I talked last night, and we want to go back up the trail to the ant spot. But this time protected, so no one gets ill. I thought you would know where we can find the right gear."

"*Señorita* Lanny, we would have to go to Panamá to purchase anything. I am thinking of another way. Miguel is a supply sergeant in the military reserves. I think if we visit him, he will be able to let us use what we need."

Four hours later, they headed back toward the *Volcán de Oro* and Miguel's ant location. This time with the gas masks Lanny wanted and the heavy gloves and lightweight rubber boots Zhou recommended.

Reassured with equipment in the car and watching the passing forest, Lanny reflected on earlier efforts to build the canal.

"Before we get there and can't talk easily because of our gear, I'm wondering if some or many of the deaths during the construction of the canal were caused by the same illness I had. Maybe they thought it was yellow fever, but it was really something else."

Zhou answered from the back seat. "Health knowledge was limited then so that they could have been wrong about the cause of worker's deaths."

Alejandro parked the Land Rover. They donned boots and masks, and Lanny stuffed her gloves in a pocket. They all took walking sticks. A tremor rattled the vehicle's door as Zhou was reaching for it. Zhou pivoted to meet the other two, eyes wide with concern.

"*Señor* Chen, this is the way this volcano is. She talks all the time but has not come to life since the Spanish conquest." Alejandro closed the door and locked the Land Rover.

"I'm getting used to this, but a geologist's promise that she's dormant would help," Lanny said, muffled in her mask.

There were no ants at their earlier place, and the bivouac was gone as well. If Alejandro hadn't recognized the location, they might have walked past without stopping.

"Hey guys, here's a crack in the soil. I remember it from yesterday." Lanny pointed at a narrow fissure winding toward them from their right. It passed across the open space where they first saw the ants disappearing under the foliage on their left.

"Did I step over an opening? I would think I would remember that," Zhou said as he wandered off on his own.

"Alejandro, on your phone, you've got a copy of the video, right?"

"*Sí, Señorita* Lanny. I can play it and show you the strange pyramid, and we can look again for the Spanish helmet." Alejandro opened his phone and adjusted some settings. Then he showed her the screen. He walked forward several steps and started turning slowly in a circle, comparing the video to what he saw. Lanny stood close by his side, following the image as well.

"Here. That is where the dead birds were. Beyond that should be the strange object, and over that way, we ought to find the helmet." Lanny's faceplate was fogging up from talking and the heat of the day, causing moist vegetation to steam as well.

They walked toward the bush, whose dark shadow masked the pyramid they saw the day before. Alejandro used his walking stick to poke at the shrub and pushed branches away from them. "*¡Mira!* A snake," he shouted as he jumped back. A Fer-de-Lance, with mouth open, wriggled from under the bush and disappeared beyond them.

Alejandro explained, "These snakes are common here, so never put your hands or feet where you cannot see them. I told you before, but it cannot be said too many times."

Lanny replied, "Wow! That's exciting. That's why I let you go first! Scary, but it wasn't interested in us, just angry at having its *siesta* disturbed." *I'd love to sic one on a couple of attorneys I know. Snake vs. snakes. OK, forget them…and pay attention.*

A TRI-CORNERED HAT?

"What happened?" Zhou re-joined them.

"Didn't you see it? A snake. It went that way." Lanny pointed and surveyed their area. "We woke up a Fer-de-Lance, and it was not pleased, but it went off to another dark spot to recover. They are beautiful, even if deadly. And fast! It zipped out of sight."

Zhou cleared a small area with his walking stick, leaned down, and picked up something.

Lanny asked, "Anything interesting?"

"No, just an unusual rock." He swatted away some bumblebees.

"OK, now that the snake is gone, can we check under the bushes?" Lanny suggested.

Alejandro gave the plant another whack with his stick for good measure and then bent down to retrieve the pyramid-shaped object at arm's length in the shadow of the bush.

He held it for inspection in a gloved hand. The three-sided object was green with moss and dingy with caked-on dirt, but it was metal.

Lanny pulled on her gloves. "Alejandro, who owns this land?"

"*Señor* Sanchez. The *Volcán de Oro* is part of the *finca*. This is our private land."

"OK, we can figure out whether we've violated any laws when we talk to Jorge. Let me hold it while you find a bag. We will need time to clean and look at it later. Right now, we should spend time on what could kill birds and make me sick."

"*Sí, Señorita* Lanny. Here is a bag. What a peculiar thing. It is like a three-cornered hat. Do you have any idea what it was for?"

"No, but it seems familiar somehow. I need to think about it for a while. There'll be a chance when we take it back and wash it."

Zhou said, "Here, let me hold it while you help with the helmet."

Lanny handed the bag to Zhou and turned to observe Alejandro carrying a disintegrating piece of metal. "Here is our helmet. It is more holes than metal. Its fragile state was not visible in the video. Another bag is essential." With careful ceremony, Lanny helped place the helmet in a protective bag.

Lanny said, "OK, now, we've got our treasures. But we still don't know what could've caused those birds' deaths. Alejandro, where were the other birds you found?"

He pointed, and the two of them wandered around the area for several minutes, stepping over fallen branches and pushing vines out of the way to search the ground. Zhou remained put, turning over the metal object in his hands as he examined it. Wandering off, he also bent over and picked up something.

Alejandro motioned to Zhou to return and spoke when they were all together. "Looking for dead birds now is not going to get us anywhere. Nothing will be here from yesterday. Some predator would have eaten them, or they would have been picked apart by the ants before dawn this morning."

Another minor quake rumbled under their feet. They looked at one another as they steadied themselves.

Lanny asked, "Do either of you think we can learn more here? What else can we do? Are we finished with our tasks?"

Zhou spoke up, "I do not think there is much to be gained by staying here. We have walked all over the terrain and even into the forest. I see nothing new. We do not know what ate the dead birds or what the dead birds ate. And I did not find ripe berries on any of the plants. The university has the soil sample and the birds. We must wait on the lab for more answers."

Alejandro nodded in agreement and added, "Not only that, but it is also almost lunchtime at the hotel. We should be going. *Señor* Sanchez has a special treat for Lanny today."

IT WAS PRIVATIZED

Zhou looked around the dining room as he waited for his solitary lunch. He watched Lanny and Jorge strolling toward the table on Jorge's private patio outside the dining area. Lanny gestured with her free hand as she spoke, the other arm entwined with Jorge's. *Perhaps she will walk with me that way, given time. I would like that.* Zhou's eyes squinted as he grinned. *Wonder what she is telling him. Perky breasts.*

"Thank you for lunch, Jorge. It was delicious. Alejandro said you had a surprise for me. I had no idea it would be so tasty." Lanny and Jorge were again seated in comfort on the small private patio.

"*Señorita* Lanny, that is only the beginning. Please, I have something to show you. I think you will enjoy the view and understand what is crucial about it."

"What in the world have you got in mind? This is exciting—and enticing." *And nice to be appreciated as a thinking person again.*

"Come with me." Rising, Jorge took Lanny's hand and headed toward a path leading away from the back of the hotel complex. Passing under an *allée* of immense Ficus trees, they came to a cleared, paved area. In the middle of the open space sat a helicopter with a giant soap bubble canopy.

"So, you're also a pilot? A man of many talents," Lanny said.

"I was a *capitán* in the *Fuerza Aérea Panameña*. After the invasion in 1989, the new regime disbanded the air force, and most of its aircraft were transferred to the civil registry."

Lanny walked to the open side of the cockpit, stood on the skid, and peered inside. "I think this is the same type of helo they used on the television show M*A*S*H."

Jorge joined her on the skid looking inside. "You are correct, *Señorita* Lanny. This is a former U.S. Army Bell OH-13 Sioux helo that somehow found its way into our squadron at the former *norteamericano* Albrook Air Force Station."

"So, was the end of the Panamanian air force something like the end of the Vietnamese air force with pilots flying aircraft out to sea, hoping to find a friendly American ship?"

Jorge answered, "Not exactly. In our case, all the flyable helos disappeared and were privatized."

Lanny reached into the cockpit and peeled off some gray paint flakes on the seat to reveal an olive drab undercoat.

Jorge stepped off the skid and removed a tie-down. "Alejandro told me you are a hang glider pilot. After he told me about your sudden illness on the volcano two days ago, I thought you would appreciate getting to know my mountain and surroundings from the air."

"Yes, an overview of the volcano by helicopter would be a real treat. Different from hang gliding where I love the wind in my face and the constant challenge of finding a landing area."

"Well, let me see if we can take it up and bring it down in one piece. Please, climb in, buckle up, and get settled while I do the walk-around and remove the other tie-downs. Your headset is on the left seat," Jorge said.

He got into the right seat, turned on the battery, and brought the piston engine to life. White smoke emerged from the exhaust, and the smell of burned aviation gasoline invaded the cockpit. As the rotor increased speed, Jorge lifted the collective to bring the light helicopter into the air—coaxing it forward as they gained speed.

In his room after lunch, Zhou couldn't resist. He opened his kit, dumped the contents, and once more held the heavy coin in his hand. *Many of these must be out there, where I found this one. No one would be there now. Time to take a drive to look for birds…round golden birds.*

Zhou grabbed binoculars and pack and headed for his car. The road and path had become familiar. He carried a sturdy walking stick, remembering the warning about snakes. Hurrying, so he would spend as little time near the volcano as possible, he came to the helmet and pyramid location faster than expected. He admonished himself while glancing around—*breathe slowly but look quickly. Must pay attention to how I feel. Look for gold.*

AN OVERVIEW

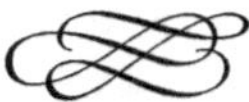

Once they were skimming the treetops, Lanny realized she had missed flying since putting her glider wing in storage several months before coming to Panama. *Why did I give up something that made me happy? Penance for losing Prez? Just too damned depressed to think? Stop this! Jorge's right. Put it away.*

Smiling at Jorge with a thumbs up, she shared her hang-gliding history and time spent aloft. "It's not powered flight like this, but I love it. It's close to being a bird, steering with my body, and chasing updrafts to glide further. Helicopter flying is also bird-like. Your ability to go low and slow, to land nearly anywhere, is magical."

Jorge thumped the instrument panel and said, "That is why I re-purposed this beauty. I wanted a way to check the condition of the forest that protects my coffee bushes. It also helps to make sure no one is logging on the far reaches of the property. There have been poachers—both of animals and trees—where we cannot easily get to them. Sadly, the canal provides a path for thieves to get away to the Pacific."

Jorge had the 'copter paralleling the slope, climbing, and maintaining a minimum height above the vegetation as they talked.

Emergent trees, many covered with white puffball flowers, stood above the level of the treetops, like taller, spotlighted sentinels.

Lanny's voice warbled to the vibration of the rotors. "This forest is remarkable. The forest canopy is unbroken as far as the eye can see, and I'm always dazzled by the number of shades of green."

"I want to show you the volcano and the extent of my ranch. First, we will go toward the Pacific, where we will be over the furthest western part of the *finca*. Then we will come back to the area where Alejandro took you earlier this morning."

"Wonderful! I love flying, and this is a luxury. It lets us see the forest details. Just like I do when I am hang gliding."

Lanny was full of questions about the forest, and Jorge was a knowledgeable naturalist, so they chatted about what they were flying over. Circling back after tracking to the end of his extensive property, he approached the old volcano's crater.

"I think these trees near the top look much less healthy than the forest we've flown over," Lanny trilled into her microphone.

"You are right. They must get less moisture than trees downhill. My coffee trees sometimes show the change from bottom to the ones on the upper slopes."

"I wonder if that's the whole reason. What if something's happening with the volcano?"

"The volcano has been sleeping for hundreds of years. Even though she now shakes, as you know, *Señora de Oro* only produces steam," he said. They flew on, and Jorge circled to the left and identified the dirt road Alejandro had taken to get her to the birding site. "It is a very small road, and it ends further toward the top of the volcano, but it is all still on my property."

Lanny pointed, "Look where the road nears that spur line on the railroad tracks. I see a car parked under a tree. Do you allow birders to come on the property without your permission? I remember a gate where we turned onto the side road. Alejandro said it just looks locked so that anyone could get up there."

"There is nothing of value up there. Just some old, abandoned buildings and the entrance to a boarded-up old gold mine. Let them wander around. Here is the next thing of interest."

FROM THE AIR CAN YOU SEE?

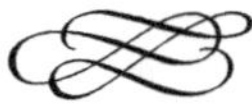

Zhou beat the stick on the bush where Alejandro had startled the snake, but nothing moved. He pushed past the shrub and stopped to examine the surroundings. Immense Giant Kapok trees shaded him, and just beyond was a staggered row whose massive trunks implied great age. At chest level, a farther tree had three deep diagonal scars. They stood out on the light trunk surface since moss and mildew had encrusted the gouges over the years, making them nearly black.

"Aah! A wild animal did not do those! I am sure a man did that. I think I am in the right place." Zhou said aloud, comforting himself with the sound of his voice. *Now where?*

Past the giant trees was a green leafy vine tangle, intimidating in scale and density. Lianas grew toward the light and wound around the nearest tree, making it impenetrable. Bumblebees circled as if they were waiting for Zhou to make a wrong move.

Zhou looked at the mound. *Need to bring tools. But now…* He swung the stick at the edge of the tangle. Nothing moved. He banged on the heap another couple of times. Still no movement. Satisfied there was no snake to disturb, he poked the cudgel into the pile, grunting when he hit something solid. *Aah, not just vines. I will come back. Soon. I need to leave now. My head is feeling strange. This place is unhealthy. Will the soil sample tell why?*

Zhou pushed branches out of the way and ducked under others, retracing his route to his car. Nearing the parking place, he was surprised to hear a helicopter's noise added to the forest's myriad sounds. *Loud—must be low.*

Below the helicopter, winding through the forest, was a pair of rails leading toward the glint of skyscrapers in the far distance. "Look, this is your history." He showed her where the railroad tracks paralleled the canal. "This was started by the *norteamericanos* before they dug the canal. They thought it could be competition for the French canal, but too many deaths made them quit. Then the French lost many workers to accidents and disease before they too gave up. The rainforest, and our landforms, was more difficult than making the Suez Canal."

"Did trains ever run on these tracks?" Lanny swiveled to take in the length of rails before they disappeared in the vegetation.

"Yes and no. The main route was the *Las Cruces* trail. My family granted a right-of-way to the Panama Railroad Company. After the U.S. took control of land and made it the Canal Zone, my family lost title until I reclaimed it when the Americans departed. The track goes all the way to Panamá, and tourists now cross the isthmus by train, but not on our tracks."

Jorge looked at the instrument panel, then turned to Lanny and said, "We own the land for miles further on, but we will turn toward the *finca* before we get low on fuel or oil."

"You thought about using the rail line for anything?"

"The family built a spur line many years ago to support the mining operation at the base of the volcano. More recently, I thought it could bring tourists who want to experience the forest and stay at the *finca*, but it is too expensive a proposition, and we don't ship enough coffee to use it."

Jorge dropped lower with the 'copter, so they were even closer to the treetops. Again, he circled to the left. "Look there. Howler monkeys are having a meal in the tree with white flowers. Some call it 'Shaving Brush Tree' for obvious reasons." The monkeys scrambled away, disliking the noise and motion. Laughing, Lanny watched the monkeys' antics as they vanished into the depths of the forest.

Remembering the second visit to the site, Lanny said, "I'm anxious to learn what Alejandro did with our two artifacts. He was going to get them cleaned up so we could identify them. Maybe he's had a chance to scrub them. You'll want to see the result as well."

"He mentioned something about an old helmet and a piece of metal, but no details. I will ask him to text me when he is meeting you. You found these on my property?"

"Yes, so actually, they are yours. We, Zhou and I, discovered them with Alejandro. I am curious about them, hoping they will give a clue to what sickened me on the side of the volcano."

"We will see what they offer. But now, the landing pad welcomes us home. What do you think of my estate? Lots of trees, no?"

As they started toward the hotel, Lanny noticed leaves caught in the helicopter's skids.

Zhou's drive back to the *finca* was uneventful. *A short rest will help rid me of this headache.* He opened the door to his room and stepped on an envelope. A message was waiting for him.

His lips moved as he whispered. "Your friend would like you to call at your earliest convenience." The only one this note could come from would be Wu Fat.

Zhou closed the door and retrieved his iPhone from a pocket, and poked the screen. "You wanted to talk to me, Master?"

He nodded and then absent-mindedly inclined his head, "I will be there."

Zhou placed the phone on the charger, kicked off his shoes, soaked a washcloth in cool water, and put it over his eyes and forehead after he lay down. It was only a matter of seconds until he was asleep, all thoughts of the cute North American birder absent from his mind.

MORE PRECIOUS THAN GOLD

Zhou was sipping tea in a nondescript Chinese restaurant three hours later, across from a Buddha-faced, round-bodied, balding man. His form may have looked like a benevolent god, but his fierce eyes killed that idea at first glance.

"As we hoped, the samples you obtained contain a high percentage of rare-earth minerals. Those will revive our computer industry and give us leverage with Panama. Now you must obtain this property so we can begin mining operations. This is a crucial assignment, and for you, a chance to make amends for the last job you had. We do not look kindly on mistakes."

"You wish me to contact *Señor* Sanchez?"

"Not just contact, convince him to sell. *Señor* Sanchez is deeply in debt. His restoration and enlargement of his hotel, the helicopter, and some unwise investments mean he is over his head and on borrowed time. Your offer, while not preferred, will be an answer to his problems...the only answer."

"Of course, Mr. Wu. I am at your service and will do anything you want. I only met *Señor* Sanchez in passing. But I am a salesman, so tell me the amount, and I will negotiate…"

"No more than one hundred American dollars per square meter and perhaps more for any useable buildings. I hope you will manage to make it much less, but the consortium authorized the maximum amount. It will be enticing since Sanchez will end up with money in the bank. No need to tell him why we want to buy it. The fewer who know, the better. Let him think we want it to provide a base for our best employees to enjoy some relaxing time and defray the cost by catering to tourists. Or, if necessary, tell him we are after gold since there is some truth in that. There is an old railway line going onto the property. We will extend it past the mine and use it to facilitate ore transport to our port facilities. We need this property at all costs."

Wu waved a pudgy hand, signaling a waiter for more water. "The first clue the rare-earth ore body is there was the illness you mentioned. It was probably from mercury. That is a common associate with those rare-earth locales. It was good the American woman got sick."

Zhou looked sharply at Wu, then dropped his eyes and concentrated on his cup of tea. He knew his boss was single-minded, focusing on the goal of wealth and power from the ore, but Lanny's illness being a "good" thing was perturbing.

"Here come our plates of noodles and juicy dumplings cooked like at home. So now, no more business. Pleasant conversation makes for happy digestion. You must tell me what you found in the forest and let us spend time savoring this meal."

WHO WEARS A MORION?

Alejandro and Lanny sat in Jorge's *casita* and sipped *Aga Vero*, a tequila liqueur. Alejandro had delayed showing off the pieces found on the volcano, building suspense as long as he could. Smiling, he opened the box and handed the helmet to Jorge.

"Alejandro, cleaning these must've been a pain, but they look so much better. Perhaps only a hundred years old now, you've subtracted eons of being out in the elements," Lanny said with a laugh. "Jorge, what do you think of your new treasure? I'm surprised the helmet isn't simply a pile of rust or whatever this metal decays to."

Jorge considered the piece he held. "The description of these two items was intriguing, but it is exciting to hold the real object. We are looking at history. This iron helmet is definitely a Spanish *morion*. The *conquistadores* wore them in the sixteenth and seventeenth centuries. The upturned edge and—*mira*—you can still see the remnant of the vertical support they called a comb. It made the helmet sturdier without adding too much weight. Also, this one had decorative designs at one time, which means it belonged to an officer. You can see something here that looks, perhaps, like a vine and leaves, but it is so worn, it is not clear. Certainly iron, not bronze, and the rust coating protected it somewhat."

Lanny asked, "What are these holes?"

"Drilled out to attach badges or decorative emblems. Observe the discoloration around the edges and," Jorge pointed to a seam, "here along the seams where the helmet was welded. This *morion* is very well preserved."

Jorge passed the helmet to Lanny and took the pyramid piece from Alejandro. "Now this," Jorge said, holding the three-sided piece, "is a bit of a puzzle. Look, it too is decorated."

"May I hold it?" Lanny set the helmet down and held out her hand for the other object. She rotated it, looked inside, and then turned it, so the object's opening was on the side. She gasped as an idea struck her.

"I think I know what this is. I said it felt somehow familiar when we first saw it. My grandmother's old trunk was a table in my dorm room and then in my first apartment for several years. It had protectors on the four upper corners. They weren't as fancy as this, but they were the exact same shape."

She handed it back to Jorge.

Jorge's eyes were bright with the lure of the chase. "I do not have a better explanation. The small holes on the edges could be to anchor it to a case of some sort. I think you are right, which leads us to the next question—where is the box or trunk it was protecting? And most interesting, what was in it?"

"The answer to that must wait until tomorrow. No treasure hunting in the dark." Alejandro said as he carefully set the helmet back in the protective box.

Jorge had a magnifying lens in hand and was examining the corner protector. "There appears to be a lion on this piece. It is badly worn, so it is difficult to be sure, but the lion on its hind legs was a symbol used by Spanish royalty forever. The lion rampant is still part of Spanish heraldry." Jorge rose and found an old leather-bound book. Then he opened it and turned the book around so that they could view it. "Here is the coat of arms for Panamá—complete with lions."

He gently placed the protector in the box. "Alejandro, thank you for the excellent cleaning job, and before we finish tonight, if you would, please rub a light coat of protective oil on these so they won't rust more and lock them in the storage room."

"*Sí, tío*, I can do that."

"But first, since your glasses are empty, let us drink a bit more *AgaVero* while we stir our brains about these old pieces of history."

NECROPSY REPORT

Lanny met Alejandro at six o'clock in the morning, as the glow of incipient sunrise was coloring the air.

"*Buenos días*. You look perkier than I feel after wine and two glasses of that wonderful *AgaVero* tequila. It's sneaky stuff. I'll bet Jorge is still asleep."

"*Sí, Señorita* Lanny. I, too, am feeling a bit not myself this morning, but we will feel better when we find some shorebirds. Today let us go to the beach. It is an hour's drive, but we can take our time and be there when the tide is coming in. You will be surprised at what birds stop in Panama as they fly to breed or escape winter."

As he finished the statement, his cell phone rang. "It is Bernardo. *Hola profesor*, what are you doing up this early? … *sí*, she and I were about to leave the *finca* to watch some shorebirds … *sí*, it is convenient for us to stop on the way … we will meet you at your lab."

Lanny looked inquisitively at him. "Did he say what news he had?"

"No, he is being clever and keeping whatever it is secret until we get there. So, we will not waste time."

The door to Bernardo's lab was unlocked. Alejandro knocked and, without waiting for a reply, held the door open for Lanny to enter first.

"Good morning, Dr. Cruz." Lanny provided him with as warm a greeting as she could muster, hoping to erase her abrupt departure the last time they were together. Alejandro stepped forward, and the two men embraced.

"Good morning, Miss Lanny, please call me Bernardo. I have a report from the university lab. Please take a seat. You too, *amigo*."

A few minutes passed with polite conversation until they were seated around a small table adjacent to the desk and computer work area. Bernardo acted as host and brought three cups of steaming coffee from a pot at the end of the work counter. Lanny smiled as she thanked him for the coffee.

"We now have the necropsy report. Here are copies for you. The birds tested positive for mercury contamination. The results on all the birds are consistent with asphyxiation by mercury vapors. Their lungs were inflamed and unable to exchange air."

Lanny spoke up. "That was what I suggested to Zhou after I spent some time researching volcanoes on the internet. It is reassuring to see my hypothesis backed up, even though it is not something I want to ever run into again."

"You were smart to be aware of the rapid change in your health and get away from the area as quickly as you did. If you had lingered, you could have ended up like one of those birds. It doesn't take long for mercury poisoning to become lethal." Bernardo's brows drew together with concern as he watched Lanny.

Looking at Alejandro, he asked, "Did you find out what the dark objects were? You remember the ones we guessed about when you were here last?"

"*Mira,* see what we found," Alejandro pulled out his cell phone and showed Bernardo photos of the cleaned artifacts. He shared the estimate of the age of the helmet and explained the corner protector. "We think the Spanish left them long before canal work started. We found them near the *Las Cruces* trail. So maybe we will find treasure as well."

"Perhaps I can join you on your next foray to the volcano and help find more clues to a treasure. At the very least, it would be a day in the field which I have not had in many weeks. Besides, I would like to search for evidence of animals living there or if the wildlife leaves this part of the mountain to avoid the fumes."

"We did find a Fer-de-Lance, so we know there was at least one very fast live creature," Lanny said, remembering the surprising speed of the snake.

Alejandro interjected, "I am spending time with *Tío* Sanchez tomorrow, but *Señorita* Lanny could show you where we were. I still have the gear Miguel loaned us so that you can be safe with masks for protection. Are you going to set live traps for animals or just look for scat and tracks?"

"Tomorrow would be acceptable to me if Miss Lanny is willing to be my guide. I will start with the simplest option. We can look for tracks and evidence of dens and whatever else might be there. I can return with live traps if it seems worthwhile." Bernardo said.

"I want to learn the answer to those questions about wildlife. I can show you where we went." Lanny sighed as she thought about a day alone with Bernardo.

They worked out details and planned to meet mid-morning when there would be maximum sunshine for tracking. After their farewells, they resumed their trip to find shorebirds. The rest of the day was uneventful for the guide and his client.

SELLING OUT?

"*Señor* Sanchez, thank you for this meeting. I am Chen Zhou, we met briefly earlier, and while I am staying here to relax and watch birds, I am also representing my company, Chinese-Panamanian Ventures. My card." Zhou bowed as they shook hands.

"Good morning, *Señor* Chen, I have heard about you from both Miss Lanny and Alejandro, and it is pleasant to see you again. I assume this meeting is not about your room since the desk did not receive any complaints. You asked for an appointment. Please, be seated and tell me what is on your mind."

Sitting in a padded chair to the side of an ornate, carved, antique desk, Zhou glanced around the spacious office. He noted the bay windows facing lush flower beds flanked by trees shading coffee bushes. Zhou directed his attention back to Sanchez.

"You have a beautiful place here, and my directors are impressed with it. CPV's presence in Panama is growing. We recently expanded operations and need to concern ourselves with the thousands of Chinese employees working here. The board is intent on keeping them happy, so homesickness does not cause resignations. It is less expensive to entertain them than to hire and train new persons." Zhou stopped to take a breath.

"Well, Mr. Chen, we will be pleased to accommodate them as guests. I'm sure we can offer you a corporate discount."

"*Señor* Sanchez, more than that, CPV would like to buy your establishment and property. We are prepared to pay well for this facility."

Jorge's eyes grew wide and then narrowed, "That offer is unexpected. I'm not sure I want to sell. I have spent years and much effort creating this beautiful place that welcomes guests like family. Like I did when you arrived."

Zhou raised a corner of his upper lip; his gold tooth glistened in the light. "*Señor* Sanchez, if we take the property off your hands, it will relieve you of any pesky debts."

Jorge's face contorted into a frown. "You appear to know too much about my business."

"On the contrary, *Señor* Sanchez, a successful businessman does his homework before making an offer on any property that has obviously seen better days. I believe the Americans call it due diligence."

Jorge squeezed his lips together and stroked his mustache. "You must understand. This land has belonged to my family for generations, and it is my life. So, it is a compliment that you think *Finca Paraíso* is special enough to entertain your employees, but it is not for sale. Not to anyone, and most assuredly not to a foreign company." He stood, indicating the meeting was over. Jorge did not extend his hand as he opened the door for the Chinese businessman.

Zhou lowered his head as he offered a slight bow and exited the office. His face remained a genial mask until Jorge closed his office door, then Zhou's lips curled unpleasantly as he remembered Wu's implied threat about failure to buy the property. He ran his damp hands down his pants and clenched them. *His life? Jorge's may be limited. A double win…if something happens to him, Lanny might pay more attention to me.*

There was no one to take note of his angry face as he stalked down the hall to his room. He picked up his binoculars and pocketed a multi-bladed tool from his suitcase.

Zhou walked out the back of the hotel towards the helicopter on its landing pad. There was no one around. He walked to it, stepped up on the skid, took out his tool, and reached inside the engine compartment.

After five minutes, Zhou said out loud, "Now, for more birdwatching on the grounds around here." He whistled softly as he stepped off the skid, turned his back on the helicopter, and wandered on the path leading toward the forest.

CAN HELICOPTERS FLY?

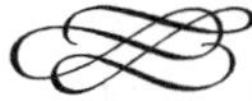

Jorge finished his third cup of coffee, wiped his mouth, and went to the helo pad. He completed his pilot's walk around, stepped on the skid to preflight the engine and cockpit, then jumped off to unstrap a tie-down.

He looked toward a shout as Alejandro ran toward the helicopter swatting his hands around his head. "These are very angry bees."

Jorge grabbed an aromatic, oily rag and waved it at the raisin-sized bees that were circling Alejandro's head. "*Sal de aquí* … get out of here."

"Ow," Alejandro shouted as he brushed something off his arm.

Jorge flapped the rag vigorously until the two men were free of the pesky insects.

"Where did they come from?" Jorge asked.

"I was cleaning my Land Rover. Some of them maybe were in it or nearby. I didn't spot them until they were all around me."

"Show me your arm," Jorge peered at Alejandro's arm and saw an angry red welt rising. "You should go inside and put something on it. Come back, and we will go for our ride."

Alejandro dashed off for first aid treatment. He was back in a flash. "*Tío, gracias.* You know I always like to fly with you. Hunting for Spanish *conquistadores* is a perfect excuse for a flight."

"And I enjoy your company. Do you remember years ago when I told you a story about how a helicopter flies?"

"*Sí, tío,* there are all these moving parts that are very different from a regular airplane."

"Yes, my son, and I told you that if you try to understand it, you will end up deciding a helicopter cannot fly. Any more than a bumblebee can fly." Jorge laughed. "We know they do but try to fathom how all those parts work together, and you will come to the conclusion a helicopter should not be able to get airborne." Jorge laughed again. "Any more than those stubby little wings on a bumblebee can possibly keep that fat body in the air."

"*Sí,* I remember. But bees fly very well, and it was an unjustified attack."

"The mysteries of bees, my boy. Neither this helicopter nor a bumblebee should be able to fly, but they do. At least this helicopter doesn't sting."

They laughed as they seated themselves in the cockpit and looked to ensure no one was near the rotor blades.

Jorge turned on the battery, adjusted his headset, and watched as Alejandro plugged into the intercom system. They tightened their seat belts and exchanged words verifying each could talk to the other. Jorge started the engine, and the blades began their slow counterclockwise rotation.

"You all set?" Jorge asked from the right seat.

Alejandro gave him a thumbs up with his right hand.

Jorge increased the throttle, and the rotor blades spun faster. Once the RPM gauge showed the blades were stable in the green, he raised the collective and fed in left pedal to counter the torque. As the skids became light and off the pad, Jorge verified that all the controls were functioning. He then pushed the cyclic stick forward and nursed the aircraft ahead in ground effect until his airspeed slowly increased to flying speed. He pulled back on the cyclic, then lifted the collective, and the bird started to climb.

They followed the dirt road from the *finca* toward the volcano. It was the same road Alejandro took when he, Lanny, and Zhou found the antbirds. When they reached the parking area, Jorge searched, looking for evidence of anything manmade. The faint trail was the only thing visible.

"*Tío*, let's go to the old gold mine. I would like to see how far the old mine is from the volcano crater."

Jorge nodded and went toward the canal until he could observe the train tracks. He then turned the helo to parallel the rails, and they followed them to a few abandoned shacks and the boarded-up entrance to a hole in the side of the hill.

"The train and this road follow the old *Las Cruces* trail, but a spur line went to the mine here," Jorge said as he hovered. He then turned the chopper to the right to give Alejandro a better view from the left seat. "*Mira*—there is the old trail continuing east to Venta de Cruces just outside of Gamboa." Jorge pushed the cyclic stick forward, and they moved along the jungle-covered trail that the Spanish once used before anyone even dreamed of a canal across the isthmus. "Most of the gold and silver took the overland route to Fort San Lorenzo on the Atlantic side, due to the threat of pirates on the Chagres River."

"*Gracias*, I had forgotten its interesting history. When was the gold mine closed?"

"The best we can tell is sometime after they built the early *norteamericano* railway along the *Las Cruces* trail, and the French arrived and started building their canal."

"We have not visited the old mine since I was a child. I want to go there again sometime."

"Of course, we can't go too far inside, but we can get a fair idea of what it was like."

"And the mine is part of the *finca*?"

"Yes, the mine, the volcano, and all our land are outside the boundary of the *Parque nacional Camino de Cruces* and the *Parque nacional Soberanía*. My land is in what used to be the old Panama Canal Zone. I don't think I told you I purchased the property after the United States left in 1979. It had been in our family for generations before they arrived, so it is most satisfactory to have the title back in our hands."

"*Tío*, did they close the mine because the gold played out?"

"*Sí*. They had been mining there since the earliest days of the *conquistadores*. Now, let's go up and look at the top of the volcano. Everyone has noticed the increasing tremors for some time now."

Jorge pulled on the collective and increased the throttle so they would climb up the slope. As they neared the summit of *Volcán de Oro*, Jorge started a counterclockwise circle around the peak. "I want to try and find any steam coming from cracks."

Alejandro looked ahead, "I don't see any steam, but I think it would be difficult with the rotor's wind." Jorge completed his tour around the top of the dormant volcano and pointed the helo's nose back toward the hotel.

EMERGENCY PROCEDURES

An angry buzzing from a bumblebee distracted Jorge. Surprised, Alejandro shouted, *"¡Cuidado!"* Jorge let go of the collective and swatted at the insect. As he released the control, his entire body felt the change in the machine. Aside from the physical sensation, there was an unexpected but definite decrease in engine noise and a change in pitch of the rotors' rotation.

Jorge looked at his instrument panel and saw the confirming rotor RPM falling. He immediately lowered the collective to maintain the RPM in the green as they descended the slope nearer to the treetops. Jorge glanced at the oil pressure gauge—zero. Oil temperature pegged at maximum.

"Engine's seized! Hang on, Alejandro. No power!" Without the engine to drive the rotor blades, they had shifted from providing lift to support flight to freewheeling, allowing air to flow from underneath and through the blades. It was not enough to keep them airborne. Jorge's emergency drill kicked in, and he prepared for an autorotation—on the volcano's uneven slope.

Nose down. Maintain sixty knots. Collective to the bottom. Keep rotor RPMs in the green. Right pedal. Jorge looked outside for flat terrain. *Need a level spot! None.* The helicopter descended rapidly as Jorge banked to the right. He spotted a flat area below on the volcano. A flat rock was sticking out. It wasn't the best location, but it was the only one. Was it wide enough to handle the skids? He hoped the steep slope would not let the rotor blades hit the side of the hill.

As the helicopter approached the intended landing area, Jorge again shouted, "Hold on. Brace yourself!"

He pulled the cyclic stick back to try to slow their descent. *Too fast. Nothing I can do.* When the skids were about fifteen feet above the rock, he leveled the nose and pulled back on the collective to cushion the touchdown. *Still too fast.* He pulled further on both controls, but the aircraft's rate of descent did not appreciably change.

Jorge's spine jarred as they thudded on the rock. He felt the skids collapse. *Maldita sea*—dammit. The aircraft rested on its bottom for a few seconds, and Jorge felt pain shoot up his back and down his arms. Then the ground gave way, and his view of the horizon tilted ominously downhill. Jorge grasped the controls with a death grip. The aircraft slid to the left—the grating of gravel on rock caught underneath the collapsed skids.

Alejandro shouted *"Tío"* as he grasped the handhold over the cabin door even as the aircraft fell on its left side, and the wooden rotor blades exploded into a thousand pieces. Dust and shattered fragments filled the cockpit. Jorge coughed and realized he could not fill his lungs. The chopper rolled over on its top, throwing Alejandro free as the aluminum frame screeched as it bent. It then slid down the incline, rolling once again, until stopping upright against a Jeep-sized boulder with a loud crash, the breaking of Plexiglas, and more screeching of bending aluminum. The acrid fumes of aviation gasoline burned Jorge's eyes.

The last thing Jorge saw and heard were shards of rotor blades flying through the broken bubble canopy and a bumblebee buzzing in front of his nose. His world went black.

PART III
UPPING THE ANTE

ALEJANDRO

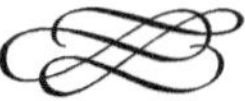

"What?" Lanny jumped when someone shook her shoulder. "Oh, I dozed off. The instruments' sounds lulled me to sleep."

The nurse shook her head, saying, *"no comprendo."* She busily checked the IV in Alejandro's arm and the levels in the bags attached to it, adjusted blankets, felt his pulse and watched the heart monitor. She nodded at Lanny and left the room.

Alejandro's head was swathed in bandages, his left arm splinted, matching the removable cast on his left leg. Lanny sighed deeply, worrying about her friend and the crises facing him when he awoke. She stood, grabbing her hands together behind her back, bending forward to loosen her back and shoulders. Satisfied with that, she walked around the room to shake out kinks. *How am I going to tell him?*

"Mmumff." Alejandro was stirring. Lanny turned to face the bed. *Perhaps a bad dream?* She hurried to the side and held his cold right hand. Alejandro's eyes fluttered, and he moaned again. She felt him pull his hand away and stepped back as he screamed a guttural cry that could be heard at the nurses' station. Lanny recovered and looked for the call button. She pushed it, and the nurse threw open the door and rushed to her patient.

"*¿Estas bien?*"

Lanny moved around the nurse so she could get a complete view of Alejandro's face. She was rewarded by seeing his puffy black and blue eyelids open. She saw his dark brown eyes focus and stare directly at her—his teeth shown as his tongue darted out and then back in. Lanny's chest caved in as she felt the breath leave her body. Her eyes filled with tears, and she knelt next to the bed and laid her head against the mattress. *He won't follow Jorge. Not another loss.*

When Lanny could think straight, she rose, took Alejandro's hand, and smiled. "Easy does it, dear friend. You've survived a pretty tough landing."

"Mmumff."

"Don't try to talk. Let me tell you what happened." She glanced around, but the nurse had left the room, and they were alone.

"You've been out since yesterday afternoon." Lanny stroked Alejandro's right hand and felt her chest heave as she attempted to gain control over her body.

"I mmumff?"

"Please, don't try to speak. I know what you must be thinking, and I will answer all your questions. Most important is that you had serious trauma, and your body needs to repair."

"Ahmmumff."

"Of course, you must be thirsty. Here—but just take a sip." She held a glass with a straw bent so he could sip, talking as he drank slowly and blinked his eyes. "Do you remember anything about yesterday when you went for the helicopter flight with Jorge?"

"Ohmumff," followed by a cough. The tiniest shake of his head said no.

Lanny kept talking while he sipped more water. "You and Jorge took the helicopter up after lunch. Something happened—they still don't know what. It crashed and rolled down the side of the volcano. You must've been thrown out, hitting some boulders with your left side. Your left arm and leg are in temporary casts, and your face is pretty colorful."

"Myumff," again followed by a cough, and this time he choked as he tried to sit up.

She set the glass on the side table and reached again for the call button.

The nurse returned with a doctor who shooed her out of the room.

A NEW REALITY

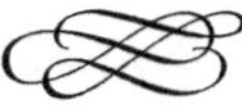

Lanny busied herself in the Clayton *Caja de Seguro Social* hospital cafeteria reading a week-old newspaper dated February 3rd. Throwing it down, she went to the counter and ordered some breakfast. After some hours, a different nurse came into the dining area and announced, "*Señor* Galvez is awake and ready to talk to you."

Lanny jumped up and hurried down the corridor to Alejandro's room. She stopped as she opened the door. Her smile reflected her relief finding him sitting up and smiling weakly. The new doctor at his side turned as the door opened and waved her in.

Alejandro's voice was still gravelly as he greeted her, "*Hola Señorita* Lanny."

Feeling like a big sister still, Lanny went to the bed and burst into tears. Alejandro's hand patted hers as she wept harder. After some time, she coughed as she shook her head. "That was too close." She looked at the doctor, who nodded. "Will he be OK?"

The doctor nodded, "*Sí, señorita.* He will mend. Talk with him for only a few minutes, and then let him rest." He departed, and Lanny turned back to look at Alejandro.

Alejandro opened his mouth and, in a quiet voice, whispered, "We went to the top of the volcano. *Tío* Jorge wanted to find any steam. You know how *La Señora de Oro* has been shaking recently. I heard Jorge shouting for me to hold on. Then lots of noise and dust." Alejandro coughed again and took a deep breath, shuddering on the intake.

"Alejandro, don't exert so much energy. Rest."

He looked up, eyes wide, "The doctor told me *Tío* Jorge is gone."

Lanny's eyes welled up. She turned her head away, took a deep breath, and said, "Oh, Alejandro, I'm so sorry he didn't survive the crash."

Alejandro's eyes and mouth opened, then closed as his head fell forward.

"I'm just heartsick." She let go of his hand and reached around his back to cradle him the best she could. She rocked him as his tears wet his gown.

The chapel's bells at the *Colegio Javier* sounded seven, bringing them both back to the present.

Lanny fought back her mourning, "The *finca* manager and I've been taking turns watching you. I was waiting for you to wake. Miguel was here too and Bernardo. You've been here for about a day and a half." She released the young man.

Alejandro looked at Lanny through wet, swollen eyes. "*Tío* Jorge was my only relative." He stopped speaking and shivered as he took a deep breath and tried to form words. "My parents and my aunt, his wife, died in an auto accident when I was young."

Lanny leaned forward to embrace Alejandro gently. "There," as she patted his back. "I feel like another auntie since I had become very fond of Jorge even though our time together was brief. He was so kind to me. He let me talk about my disappointments and fears from work. There was an instant rapport and such affection…"

His muffled voice was only just understandable. Lanny strained to hear him. "He raised me alone. I barely remember my father. *Tío* is truly my father. Was—he was like a father."

"There's no one else we should notify?"

"No." He took a shaky breath. Alejandro held his ribcage as he breathed out. His pain and the stress of tears were evident to anyone—fatiguing. His eyelids drooped, and he closed his eyes.

Lanny knew he had drifted off again, hearing raspy snoring. Lanny sat, thinking, as the heart monitor and IV's rhythmic sounds provided a backdrop to Alejandro's troubled sleep.

"Hello, *Señorita* Lanny."

Lanny looked up at Zhou's smiling face and wondered if his gold tooth was solid or just plated.

"I heard an unfortunate rumor that our host died in a helicopter crash." Zhou leaned over the table where she was having a late meal. "Is it true?"

"Yes, it's true. Alejandro was with him and was also injured." Zhou's gold tooth gleamed in the candlelight from the table. Looming over her, she felt threatened, like being cornered by a feral animal.

Still smiling, Zhou nodded, "It seems hard to believe. I was talking with *Señor* Jorge just about lunchtime the day of the unfortunate accident."

"It really is hard to believe that Jorge is gone. He was so alive. So much a force that you would assume he'd be here for a very long time."

Zhou's smile disappeared. "Well, I merely stopped to determine if the rumors were true. Since Alejandro is indisposed, would it be correct for me to give you his fee?"

"Indisposed? I guess you could say that—or perhaps more accurately, lucky to be alive! I'll be glad to take his money to him. I'm spending time at the hospital. Jorge was his nearest relative." Lanny trembled and thought how inappropriate this conversation was becoming.

"Ah, taking him the money would be helpful." Zhou fumbled in his wallet and handed several bills to Lanny. "This covers what we agreed on, plus a tip. Please extend my sympathy regarding *Señor* Jorge to Alejandro. I will leave you to finish your meal. It appears this accident ended any immediate plans for more birding together. Perhaps we will cross paths again."

"You're right. My birding is shelved for now. Alejandro is a friend, and I need to help him." Lanny sensed there was something more that Zhou was not sharing. "I'll give him your regards."

"Jorge was Alejandro's relative? I thought he was only called *tío* as a courtesy."

"Good question Zhou. Their relationship was much more than an honorary title." She watched him leave the room, wondering why she felt edgy.

WE WANT ANSWERS

L anny quietly opened the door, hoping Alejandro was finishing a peaceful night's rest. Her face lit up when she saw him sitting with an empty breakfast tray and looking alert.

"Wow. This is better than I expected. I thought you would be down for several more days. You've got quite a rainbow on your face, but the swelling is almost gone. So how are you feeling?"

"*Señorita* Lanny! Good morning. I am improving by the minute. The best news is that my leg has a hairline fracture, not a break. The worst news, of course, is that *tío* is still dead. I do not want to believe it. It will be very different without him."

"You'll have challenges with Jorge gone, but you're capable. You've already had experience as his *protégé*. I've watched you in action. It'll take time, but you'll be fine. Right now, I hope you can help me figure out what happened."

"But of course, I too want to know about the crash. How can I help?"

"I was in that helicopter the day before. It was old, and Jorge may've been a casual pilot, but he was skillful, and he did a thorough pre-check, so the accident is strange."

Alejandro leaned into his pillows and closed his eyes. "I have unconnected images but ask, and I will try to remember what happened."

Lanny clarified while Alejandro was thinking. "Bernardo was with me when we heard the crash. We had just set two box traps. The noise was so loud we thought something was on top of us. We figured it was a plane, and we ran to his Jeep. From the small, bare area on the volcano flank, we could see smoke or dust—whatever it was, above us on the volcano."

Alejandro nodded.

"By the way, Bernardo said he would be by this morning. He thinks he saved your life, so he wants to know how you are today." Lanny had to force herself not to smile when she thought about being with Bernardo again.

Alejandro opened his eyes, frowned, and said, "Jorge wanted to see if there was steam or smoke from cracks since there has been so much shaking lately. We flew around the top of the volcano. We did not find any steam and then headed back to the *finca*. I remember the silence. No! There was a bee! *Tío* tried to set us down on a flat spot. He told me to hang on." Alejandro choked up and stopped, so Lanny re-started her story.

"Bernardo drove like a maniac up the track toward the plume of smoke. He used his machete, blazing a trail after we got close with the Jeep. I called the emergency number on his phone to get medical help fast. Then we just pushed through the forest toward where we thought the smoke was coming from."

"*Tío* said something about the engine quitting, 'seizing' was the word. I don't know what it grabbed, but it stopped. Then we tipped when we touched down, and the blades broke and flew in like razors. *Tío* screamed, and I couldn't hang on." Alejandro buried his head in his hands. "Lanny, he's really gone." Alejandro sobbed.

She squirmed in her seat at the edge of his bed, feeling helpless. She wiped her clammy hands on her jeans and debated about leaving. She was starting to move when the door swung wide, and Bernardo entered. Lanny could not help herself and gave Bernardo her best smile.

He quickly returned a big smile and wink before concentrating on his friend. Patting an unbandaged knee, he said, "Alejandro! Good to see you, young man. I thought you'd be in casts up to your nose, but you look like you can swim the canal tomorrow. Sorry about your *tío*. He was a great man and a good friend to me. I know you loved him like a father."

"*Gracias* Bernardo, although he was not really my father, he raised me like a son."

"We need to get you up and move so you can pay your respects and say goodbye." Bernardo turned to Lanny. "*Buenos días*, Lanny. Thank you for keeping Alejandro company. He needs the distraction."

"Hi." She said, reflecting his cheerful attitude. "You're right. He looks like he's going to live." Lanny re-directed her smile at Alejandro.

"I am going to survive," Alejandro squinted as he looked at his two friends—determination in his voice.

Lanny continued, "I've been quizzing him about the crash, trying to find out exactly what happened. The bump on his head hasn't helped his memory. He can only recall bits and pieces." She looked at Bernardo, "Maybe you can say something that will help bring another piece back. He remembers a bee in the helo and silence. Jorge said the engine seized. What does that mean?"

"I'm not a pilot, but that means the engine suddenly froze up. The most usual cause for an automobile engine seizing is a problem with lubrication—running out of oil. I had that happen once with an old vehicle. I hit a rock on a rough road and punctured the oil pan without realizing it. When the oil drained out, the engine seized."

Alejandro closed his eyes for a few seconds and said, "That must be it."

Bernardo added, "Although Jorge was a bit careless with things, he was pretty safety conscious. I would be surprised if he'd let the oil go low, let alone dry. There must be a reason the oil was low."

Lanny asked, "Could it've been an accident, or might someone have caused the problem?"

"Let me text my friend Marcos. He's leading the crew who are bringing the wreckage off the volcano. He's also a former *Fuerza Aerea Panamena* helicopter pilot … currently an accident investigator for OFINVAA. That stands for the *Oficina de Investigación de Accidentes Aéreos*, a part of the *Autoridad de Aeronáutica Civil*. Your version in the States is the NTSB. Here, they are a small and overworked bureaucracy. So, they are slow like snails. We can ask Marcos to look at the obvious while they get organized. As a former pilot, he knows not to screw things up."

Alejandro and Lanny talked about how soon he could leave the hospital while Bernardo stood next to the window and thumbed a text. "OK, that's on its way. Whatever he finds, knowing the situation with the engine oil is important." Bernardo put his hand on Alejandro's shoulder. "You were talking about wanting out of here. Get some rest, and perhaps we can spring you tomorrow."

Bernardo and Lanny sat in the hospital cafeteria. Bernardo broached his thoughts about the crash. "What if the crash is also somehow related to the problem you brought to me—those strange bird deaths. That feels so long ago, but could this tie to that episode?"

"I'm not sure I want to relive the experience of finding the helicopter and both men. I can't think how mercury vapors could do anything to a helicopter or its pilot at height." She shuddered, seeing too well the wreckage and bloodied bodies. Then, fearing they had found two corpses, there was the relief of getting a pulse on Alejandro, only to find Jorge had none.

"We hadn't finished our thorough inspection of the area where we put the traps. It's only ten thirty; why don't we use the rest of the morning to revisit the vapor site and find out if we caught anything? We can also go to the crash location if you are OK with that. I still have the protective gear in the Jeep. Do you have any other plans?" He smiled and put his hand on hers.

Lanny felt her face flush. She turned her head down so Bernardo could not observe her reaction to his touch. "One more sip of coffee, and I'm ready to go. Besides, don't you need to see if there are critters in your traps?"

Zhou looked at the Buddha-faced, balding man seated across from him. "Master Wu, I have eliminated one problem. Jorge wouldn't sell, and now he is no longer a factor. It's not even clear who is the new owner until the will is examined, and we learn who inherits." Seated once again in Wu Fat's favorite Chinese restaurant, Zhou reported his success with some relish. He tried to camouflage his pain and ignore the beads of perspiration that broke out on his forehead from the Kung Pao Shrimp Wu Fat had ordered for them.

Wu Fat asked, "What if there is no will? Then we will have to wait to see if the State takes over the property and sells it for back taxes."

"Yes, that might take longer, but we could obtain the property at a significantly lower price." Zhou paused to wipe his brow. "But perhaps we need to move more quickly. A few well-placed Balboas in the hands of the right people could give us what we want sooner. The State would auction off the property for the price of some back taxes."

"That remains true only as long as no one knows about the rare-earth deposits. Those are worth many millions of dollars and would change the whole equation. They must remain our secret. It is time to put pressure on some lawyers and find out what is in the will." Fat's jaws worked feverishly on a bite of food.

Wu Fat asked, "And our plan if Alejandro inherits?"

"Alejandro is simply a guide for people who want to watch birds. I didn't observe any ambition to own or run the *finca* when I was with him. He seems content with his life as it is. But even if he decides he wants the property, he will not possess the resources to pay the back taxes. He should be easy to convince to sell so that he won't have the headache of the place and its debt," Zhou said.

He continued, "After the purchase of the *finca*, we will be able to refurbish and extend the rail line into the area of the volcano and the rare-earth deposits. That will give us fast, secure transport. We will be able to ship the ore to the new refinery near David (pronounced Dahveed). That facility should be able to purify enough to satisfy our own computer requirements."

"You remember I found an old gold coin and other Spanish artifacts. We can use gold as an excuse for our mining activities and rail activity."

"That is an excellent suggestion. I like it. A diversion that will cause anyone snooping to think we are merely looking into re-opening an old gold mine."

Zhou pictured himself riding his master's coattails up the organization. His vision included sharing his success with the cute American birder.

Wu Fat said, "We can ship from our docks in Panamá. It will be a great coup and make us honored in China when we accomplish this. We will be second to none in our ability to drive the international computer markets. I'll bet we can put those refineries in Malaysia out of business."

"And what about our plans for Costa Rica?"

Wu Fat smirked and said, "That is why we will extend the rail lines even further north. To link up with another refinery just over the border." He spoke through another mouthful of Kung Pao, "Now, obtaining the acreage is critical and the first priority. You will talk with our lawyers tomorrow and get firm answers on who inherits and plan our next steps." Wu Fat cooled himself with a heart-shaped palm-leaf fan.

ZHOU'S TRUE COLORS

Armed with a sheaf of papers arranged by Wu Fat's stable of lawyers, Zhou stopped at the hospital information desk. "Alejandro Galvez's room, please." He raised an eyebrow at the attractive young woman behind the counter.

"Second floor, this wing, number seven," she responded in English.

"Thank you, *señorita*," he inclined his head and headed for the elevator glancing behind him to get another view of the receptionist from the side.

The door to number seven was open, and Alejandro, dressed in street clothes, was sitting on the edge of the bed.

"Good morning, Alejandro. You appear well," Zhou said as he entered.

"Hello, Zhou. I'm hoping to get released very soon. I will heal the rest at home. Lanny gave me the money you sent. Thank you for your concern that I get it," he replied.

"Well, aside from seeing for myself that you are getting better, money is precisely the reason I am here. I understand that you will inherit the *finca*."

"Yes, my uncle made a will with me, the executor and sole beneficiary. I will inherit his estate. That includes the *finca*."

"As the new owner, I know you will have to meet the demands of those excessive past taxes on the property. You are going to need money to avoid a delinquent tax sale. You know, if you cannot pay them."

"Will I be required to do that right away?"

"This is Panama, and you know things do not move quickly. But eventually, you will need to settle the taxes. The company I work for authorizes me to make an offer for the *Finca Paraíso*. I was speaking with your uncle about this just before the tragic and unfortunate accident. He seemed quite interested in the proposal, and I believe he was considering selling. He said he was tired of the *finca* losing money and being strapped for cash." Zhou stopped talking and watched Alejandro wince when private family business was mentioned.

Alejandro stood, favoring his sore leg by hanging on to the bed frame, "I know *tío* was having financial trouble, but he had not mentioned selling the *finca*. He loved the land and what he was doing to get the bottom line back into the black. I can't believe he would think of giving it up."

Zhou continued, "Jorge was getting older, maybe getting tired, and perhaps that was part of his reasoning. Coffee prices have been fluctuating, and we recognize the *finca* will need an influx of cash to finish the projects Jorge started. I don't know what was behind his considering our offer, but he said he would think about it."

"What do you plan to do with the property if I sell it?"

"Our company can save money by using the *finca* as a recreational facility for our workers. It will be cheaper than flying them back to China or hiring new people to replace unhappy employees."

Alejandro lifted his working arm and gently felt the unshaved stubble on his chin.

Zhou pressed on, "I know it's soon to speak of it again, but the company is in a hurry, and nothing is to be gained by waiting. Let us help you by taking these financial problems off your hands and provide you with enough money to live comfortably for the rest of your life."

Alejandro's brows drew down, "This is a surprise. It adds to the shock of losing my uncle. I too must think about this offer, and of course, I need to talk with the manager of the *finca*. He is the one with the knowledge of debts and what *tío* might have been thinking."

"This offer won't wait forever, and the sum is quite generous. I suggest you make time to consider our proposition. I will leave these papers for your examination, and I'll check back with you soon." Zhou laid the sheaf of papers on the end of the bed and took a couple of steps toward the door. "You don't want another accident," he hissed softly.

At that moment, Bernardo filled the doorway. He started to smile, then recoiled to avoid bumping Zhou. His raised eyebrow told Zhou he'd been heard. He bowed, scooted past Bernardo without speaking, and strode briskly out of sight.

"Hey, I get here to finally bust you out of this place, only to find Zhou, acting like some *matón*, making a clear threat. What was that all about?"

"I'm still trying to absorb it. Let's get out of here, and we can talk."

"*Bueno*. I have lots of news. Some about your crash, and I'm putting pieces together. And there is good news as well. Let me tell you what happened after Lanny and I returned to the volcano."

SHOULD WE TELL ANYONE?

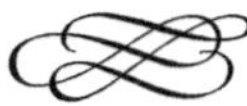

"Lanny, we ought to be going to talk more about our discovery with Alejandro. Before we take examples to show him, I want to warn you since I'm having difficulty believing Zhou is a simple Chinese businessman. Yesterday I heard him threaten Alejandro."

"What?" The hot coffee cup tipped in Lanny's hands, spilling the contents on the laboratory tabletop. "Damn!"

Bernardo continued talking as he grabbed towels at the lab sink.

"Alejandro told me Zhou made him an extremely lucrative offer for the *finca* then tried to scare him when he did not immediately accept."

"Scare him how?" Lanny wiped up the spilled coffee with paper towels.

"With another 'accident.' The more I hear, the more it appears there is more to the crash than an accident. There was no reason for a rupture in that oil line."

Lanny paused to think through what they had heard from Marcos, the OFINVAA investigating team, and what she learned from searching the internet. "And you think Zhou could've been involved? I'll admit he makes me very uneasy, but to sabotage the helicopter?"

"Can't be sure. But if the Chinese want the *finca*, how far might they go to get control?"

"Was the offer legitimate?"

"Quite generous—one hundred American dollars per square meter plus twice the going rate for the hotel and other buildings."

"That's too complicated for my non-metric mind."

"Let's say it is twice what any other property like this sold for in the past few years."

Lanny whistled. "What's Alejandro going to do?"

Bernardo shrugged his shoulders. "*No sé*. The *finca* always needs work, and Jorge let some preventative maintenance slide this last year. He also had some debts and is behind on the property taxes."

"Are there inheritance taxes here as well?"

"No, but Alejandro is going to be hard-pressed to come up with the money to pay off the debts and property taxes."

Lanny deposited the wet paper towels into a receptacle. "So, he might sell."

"I'm afraid so."

"Is there anything we can do to delay the sale? Our find will take time to help him. How about the environmental dangers due to mercury vapors?"

"Hmm, that could be a useful reason." Bernardo hesitated, then sat at his computer and began to tap keys. Lanny came over and stood behind his chair.

"Look at this, Lanny. The fumes and problems we have observed at the *Volcán de Oro* are consistent with volcanic activity in other parts of the world. The problem is there is no obvious volcanic activity near the *finca*."

Lanny leaned forward to take in the screen more clearly. "Try searching for plate tectonics instead."

Bernardo clicked keys displaying new websites as fast as most men click through television channels with a remote. "*Mira*, the results of a plate shift could be some minor rumbling—earthquakes and escaping gases to include mercury vapor."

"So, the land might be an environmental disaster area in need of remediation—you know, clean-up."

"That could be very costly. Alejandro could not begin to fund what might be required."

They both paused and took in deep breaths.

Lanny broke the silence. "Maybe Alejandro ought to just get rid of the property and not look back."

WHAT CAN YOU LEARN FROM A BUG?

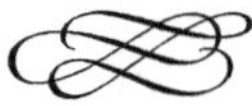

Zhou closed the passenger door on the silver Mercedes-Benz S-Class sedan. "Good morning, Master Wu."

Wu Fat looked at Zhou and scowled. "I trust you have pleasing news?"

"A thousand pardons, honorable Master." Zhou bent and humbled himself as best he could in a car's passenger seat worth three times the average Panamanian income. "The young man remains undecided."

"And what incentives did you offer?"

"As you instructed, Master Wu. A price more than twice the estimated value."

"And what dangers did you warn him of?"

"His problems with the government if he cannot pay the taxes and the possibility of another accident."

"And he did not take you seriously?"

"Master, I was interrupted by the professor from the university."

"Perhaps it is time for a follow-on visit where this young man will be made to understand what is in his best interests."

"Of course, Master. But there have been some new developments."

"Yes, what?"

"This professor and Ms. Mitchell were talking yesterday and have concluded that there is an environmental problem at the volcano that needs remediation."

"That would be the mercury vapor?"

"Yes, Master. Ms. Mitchell quickly realized that *Señor* Galvez would not possess the resources to deal with the problem."

"Her recommendations?"

"Either go to the government or sell the land without disclosing the problem."

"Just how did you come by this information?"

"Master, on my earlier visit, I pretended to drop something and left behind a voice-activated bug in Professor Bernardo Cruz's office. I tasked one of my associates to monitor the recordings and send me transcripts."

"Excellent work. I think with what we know of Ms. Mitchell, she will lean towards taking the problem to the government. After all, she is an environmental lawyer, right?"

Zhou answered, "Yes, as contained in the dossier I provided you."

"Well, if she thinks she will get any help from the government, she will learn she is mistaken. We still have all the right players in our pockets, do we not?"

"Yes, Master. We took care of everyone with any oversight when we applied to build the high-speed rail line to David."

"So, we can rule out any government interference and perhaps be more aggressive in our approach to *Señor* Galvez."

"Master, what if we offer to take the property with the known environmental issues and use that to our advantage?"

"How so?"

"We will employ massive earth-moving equipment to extract the rare-earth. How would anyone know whether our activities are remediation or excavation?"

"I like the way you are thinking, Zhou. Perhaps I have underestimated you."

Zhou felt his face burn, and he again turned his head down in the semblance of a humble position.

"Give the young man, Alejandro, one more chance to see it our way. Use whatever technique you think will help him decide."

"Of course, Master Wu."

Wu Fat looked directly into Zhou's eyes. "But if he still does not budge, then kill him."

RARE-EARTH

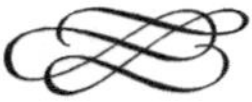

Bernardo pulled out the chair for Lanny. "I think you will enjoy the meal."

Lanny sank into the comfortable chair. "Chef's table at Caliope? My God, I've wanted to eat here ever since I learned of this place."

"Being an academic in Panamá comes with benefits." Bernardo sat opposite Lanny and then rose again as the chef approached.

"*Buena noches, Profesor* Cruz," the chef exaggerated the title with a grin.

Retaliating, Bernardo emphasized his introduction as well, "*Señor* Martin Pace, may I present *Señorita* Pamela Mitchell."

Lanny extended her hand, "Please call me Lanny." She smiled at their exchange as she appraised the young man in his double-breasted black chef's coat.

Martin bowed and brushed Lanny's hand with his lips. "*Encantado.*"

"Martin, please make our evening one to remember." Bernardo embraced his friend. Martin smiled as he again bowed, this time with a theatrical flourish, did an almost-military about-face and disappeared toward the kitchen.

"Our families have known each other for many years, and I have watched and supported his ability and growing fame. Now he can experiment. He has introduced a farm-to-table dining experience—new to Panamá."

"The friendship you share is obvious. I'm excited to see what he creates."

While they waited for their wine to arrive, Lanny remarked on the floral arrangement's beauty at their table. Bernardo explained they were the national flower of Panama, a white orchid known as the Flower of the Holy Spirit.

After they touched glass rims together, he said, "Lanny, I looked into what might be of so much value that the Chinese are willing to pay top dollar and why Zhou would threaten Alejandro."

"Chen gives me the creeps without a good reason. Is he thinking about the old gold mine? That doesn't seem tremendously valuable."

"Yes, and there are always rumors of buried treasure. However, I became intrigued by the geology associated with dormant volcanos."

Lanny searched her mental inventory of stored information as she gently swirled her glass. "I'm drawing a blank. What did you learn?"

"Some igneous rocks and pegmatites, and perhaps lateritic soils, are associated with rift zones. These, including dormant volcanos, can be a source of several things, rare-earths among them. Those are used to manufacture smartphones, digital cameras, computer parts, and in the renewable energy technology industry, military equipment industry, glass-making, and metallurgy."

Lanny nodded. "So, we have a large and growing need for minerals and ore most people haven't heard of."

He looked pleased with her understanding. "That fits what we seem to be facing. There are some twenty-one rare-earth minerals, and yes, most people have probably never had reason to hear of them, even though some drive their computers and their cell phones." He poured more wine into both of their glasses.

Lanny said, "I've read that not too long ago, China replaced the U.S. as a major source for rare-earth minerals. If there is an unexpected commercially valuable deposit here, that could be a hidden incentive to get the property. Perhaps mercury as well since we've had experience with that. As an environmental lawyer, I could defend those possibilities, even if it does no good against expensively-bought 'expert' witnesses who won because no one would listen to me."

"You sound angry. Is that a partial explanation of your being here?"

"I didn't mean to go there; it's the wine speaking. The short version is yes, that's part of it. Another part of being here is running from loss. I couldn't prevent the deaths of people I loved. Before Jorge, my grandmother, who raised me and was my confidant, recently died." *And my lover also, but I can't talk about him, especially not to you.*

"I may tell you the whole sad story another time. Right now, I'm curious about what we may have found. And then, I want to devote myself to enjoying our meal and this evening."

"OK, this last thing tonight. Rare-earth minerals found in concentration make mining economically feasible. The Chinese dominate the market, using resources in Outer Mongolia. But everyone fears the existing supply will be exhausted within the next ten years—even less if technology continues to expand into non-traditional markets."

"And if the *finca* is a new source for the Chinese?"

"Then, it could explain why they want to enlarge their stable of properties in Panama."

"So, what should Alejandro do? Sell to the Chinese or seek another backer to explore and extract the rare-earth elements if they exist?"

"Lanny, I think the reason the Chinese made such a generous offer is they already know there is rare-earth material on the property. I think Alejandro could come out way ahead if he holds on to the property and tries to find a better deal. Shall we drink to that?"

Bernardo's comment could not have been better timed. Their first course arrived, and they clinked their glasses again.

A leisurely meal later, Zhou watched the pair leave Caliope, and he signaled the waiter for his check. He removed the earpiece and sneered as he thought how inexpensive the orchids were compared to the information they helped him learn this evening. And fortunate that his bug in Bernardo's office allowed him to learn of their dinner plans, even if it made him angry when he thought about Lanny's response to him.

Zhou walked to his car and fumbled with his iPhone. "Hello, this is *Señor* Chen. Did you obtain the item I requested?"

IT'S NOW OR NEVER

In the dark, at the back of the hotel, Zhou opened the hood of Alejandro's Land Rover and placed a cardboard box to the side of the engine block. He then removed two fuel injectors and directed their output into holes in the cardboard box. He cut the string surrounding the box once the box appeared solidly set. He closed the hood making sure that nothing tilted. Zhou then went to his car in a far corner of the hotel parking lot and plugged in his earpiece. He had an unobstructed view of the Land Rover and time for a nap while he waited.

Lanny and Bernardo sat waiting for Alejandro in Jorge's former office.

"What's keeping him?" Lanny asked, not expecting an answer.

"Nothing," Alejandro replied, limping as he came through the doorway.

Bernardo stood and extended his hand in a greeting that turned into a welcome hug.

After also standing for a hug, Lanny sat and asked, "You've gone over the finances with the *finca* manager and a tax attorney?"

"*Buenos días* to you both," the young man stated as he maneuvered past his guests to the big chair behind the desk. "OK, now to work. I have done my, as you *estadounidenses* say, due diligence. And thank you for providing the information about the rare-earth minerals."

"So, what's it going to be?" enquired Bernardo.

"I cannot bring myself to sell the property. It has been in the family since the time of the *conquistadores*."

Lanny jumped to her feet and pumped her clenched right fist. "Terrific. What are your plans? What can we do to help? We're in this with you."

Waving his arm to calm her down, Bernardo chuckled and asked, "And how about the rare-earth?"

Alejandro answered, "My advisors tell me that we need to deal with the government and obtain mining permits. They don't think this will be a problem. Once the government understands there is a potential for major economic development, they will delay action on delinquent taxes until we obtain financial backing for our operations."

Bernardo asked, "And what about the Chinese?"

Alejandro looked at the desktop and picked up some documents stapled to a blue cover. "*Mira*—the latest." He handed the papers to Bernardo.

Bernardo reviewed each page and then handed them to Lanny. "An even better offer than last time."

Lanny put the papers back on the desk and asked, "When did you get these?"

"Zhou was here about an hour ago. He said it was their final offer."

"He knows you said no?"

"Yes, when he left here, he clearly understood that the property would only be sold over my dead body."

Bernardo added, "Let's hope it does not come to that."

Alejandro beckoned to the door. "Lanny. Professor Cruz. Let's go out to the area of the old gold mine. I want to show you something I found yesterday."

They went out to the Land Rover and got in. Alejandro turned the starter and stopped when the engine did not catch as expected, and there was a distinct smell of gasoline.

"What the …" Alejandro said. He motioned toward the ignition key but was interrupted by Bernardo's hand on his arm.

Bernardo said, "Wait! Don't try the starter again. Something might catch fire. I smell gasoline, possibly a break in a fuel line. Let's look under the hood."

The three of them got out of the vehicle and approached the front. The smell of gasoline was quite pronounced. Alejandro reached for the latch and opened the hood.

"What is that doing there?" Lanny asked.

Bernardo glanced at both as he answered, "There is no logical reason for a cardboard box with holes to be in the engine compartment. Let alone with fuel injectors fed into the box. Let's get some long-handled tools and take it out. Drop the hood."

They grabbed rakes and a shovel from the nearby tool shed and returned to the Land Rover. Carefully raising the hood, Bernardo used a rake to hold down the lid while he removed the fuel injectors from the box's small holes.

"Alejandro, you put your shovel under the box and see if you can lift it. Lanny, you put your rake up in the air and start swinging if anything comes out."

Alejandro lifted the box and bent over to place it on the ground. As he did so, the top of the box flew up, and a gasoline-soaked Fer-de-Lance sprung out, mouth wide open, fangs ready to strike.

"Lanny, get it!" Bernardo yelled.

Lanny swung down at the viper and caught it mid-body. Bernardo pushed his rake on the head of the snake, and Alejandro swung his shovel and cut it off.

At the other end of the parking lot, Zhou winced—both for the snake and himself.

THE PENALTY FOR FAILURE

Wu Fat did not look pleased. "Tell me again why you failed in your tasking?"

"Honorable Master Wu, there are no excuses."

"That is correct. You have dishonored yourself, the company, the government, and the Han people."

"A thousand apologies, Master."

"A thousand apologies do not make up for purchasing a Fer-de-Lance with a company credit card and leaving it in the original box. How soon do you think it will be before the authorities trace the sale to you and show up at our doors?"

"I will never make such a mistake again."

"No, you will not."

Two black-hooded men entered the room from the side. Zhou knew what would happen and resolved not to embarrass himself in front of Wu Fat or his henchmen. Like with many other things in his life, Zhou failed. He felt his bowels empty down his trouser legs. He closed his eyes as he heard the swishing of a blade. He felt the sharp pain on the side of his neck. As he lost consciousness, his last thoughts were of the beautiful birder from North America, her perky breasts, and his shame.

A REVEALING LUNCH

"Chen Zhou left his room after our talk and has not been seen at our hotel for several days," Alejandro remarked to the pair sitting with him on the patio at the *finca*. "Because I filed a complaint about the snake, the police checked his passport against departures. He has not left the country—at least not by air."

Bernardo raised an eyebrow. "What about ships? Today we see them carrying shipping containers. For a price, many of those carry an occasional passenger."

Nodding, Alejandro said, "It's harder to check with those ships since so many come through the canal each day, but the authorities are trying. They also put the airlines on alert and will let me know if he is apprehended. Then I can decide if it is worthwhile to press charges."

The whisper of a breeze carried the aroma of Star Jasmine to Lanny. Time slowed. *Just breathe. It's good now.* Taking a deep breath, she looked over Alejandro's shoulders at the flowers. *What changes since the last time I sat here with Jorge. He would be so pleased with Alejandro's growth—and what I get to tell him.* Her grin at the two men hinted at her excitement.

Beaming at Alejandro, she said, "It's so beautiful here, and making it better, Bernardo and I have a surprise for you. We flipped a coin —this one," she said, palming it before he could see it, "and I get to tell you." She paused to take a breath.

"Tell me what?"

"Bernardo and I finally got back to the slope of the volcano where we discovered the ants that started all the excitement. We were thinking about what caused the—what we assume is mercury poisoning and the interest by Zhou in the area."

Bernardo swiveled in his chair and frowned exaggeratedly. "Will you hurry up, or must I tell him? This is agony."

"OK, OK, we found something that isn't related to gases or rare-earth or gold or whatever else might be mined. On second thought, it is related to gold…" While she hesitated, Bernardo reached over and grabbed her hand.

"Just show him," he said, extending her arm toward Alejandro.

She uncurled her fingers, exposing an ancient gold piece. "After dislodging one more Fer-de-Lance, we poked around and uncovered chest remnants that must've belonged with the corner piece we found."

"*Madre de Dios!*" His eyes wide, Alejandro gingerly took the coin from Lanny's hand, and his chin trembled as he contemplated it.

Bernardo held on to Lanny's hand while he added. "There are many more just like this, and also other relics. If you manage the contents well, even with the percentage the government will take, you are finished with any financial troubles."

His eyes brimming with tears, Alejandro put the coin on the table and covered it with his hand. "If only *tío* were here to see this. This will finish the projects and make the *finca* secure."

WHAT COMES AROUND

Caliope's chef Martin smiled at Bernardo and Lanny as he escorted them to an impressive dining room reserved for small parties of affluent guests. He extended his hand in greeting to the third member of the dinner group.

Bernardo made the introduction. "Chef Martin Pace, this is *Señor* Alejandro Galvez. We think Alejandro is going to be one of your frequent and influential customers."

"Of course." The chef turned to face Alejandro. "*Señor* Galvez, I have read about you in *Mi Diario* over the past months. Is it all really true?"

Lanny watched Alejandro blush and stutter as he tried to answer. "Poor Alejandro. This newfound notoriety is difficult for him. He will eventually get used to fame and fortune."

Bernardo jumped in. "Martin, let's not embarrass Panama's newest and most honest millionaire more than we already have. Just assume everything you read in the newspaper is more or less correct."

"Of course. *Señor,* we are delighted you are visiting our restaurant." Martin considered that his opportunity to withdraw. He asked on the way out, "One more for dinner, correct?"

Bernardo said, "Yes, someone will be joining us shortly." He smiled at both, lingering on Lanny, as the waiter poured ice water in tall, frosted glasses.

Lanny turned to her fellow birder and said, "Alejandro, you should be proud of yourself. With both the rare-earth discovery and the gold, you are single-handedly bringing great economic wealth to your nation. Not to ignore the share that will be given to you." Her voice rose slightly, "What was exciting to me was finally completing the riddle of the Spanish artifacts with Bernardo. No more snakes where we first found the old pieces, but instead a treasure chest filled with Spanish gold *escudos,* several lovely jewelry pieces, and beautiful icons."

Alejandro held up his water glass in a pretend toast. "And more gold now with the resumption of mining at the old mine at *Volcán de Oro.* All of this paid off the debts and for even more improvements to the hotel."

Alejandro soberly added, "And the new bird sanctuary adjacent to the *Parque nacional Camino de Cruces* named *Jorge Sanchez de Pinos Sanctuario de Aves.* And the *Parque nacional Soberanía* will continue to protect birds and other animals and bring in eco-tourism dollars."

Alejandro looked quizzically at Lanny, "Are you sure you want to live here as an ex-pat? You could keep the profits from our partnership and live in the States."

"Yes, I'm staying here. I've fallen in love with the country and its people."

Lanny smiled at the handsome academic and added, "Bernardo and I discovered we work well together, and he has revived my interest in studying animal populations. That's something I took very seriously in college. The degree in Zoology got superseded by environmental law, but I can indulge in the renewal of interest since I've left Carter, King, and Chavez behind!

A shapely Panamanian beauty who was the restaurant's hostess entered the small dining room and announced, "*Señorita y Señores*, your fourth for dinner has arrived. May I present Mr. Wu Fat?"

GLOSSARY

allée − an alley in a formal garden or park, bordered by trees or bushes.

amigo − friend.

Autoridad de Aeronáutica Civil − Panamanian national Civil Aeronautics Authority.

buenas días − good day.

buenas noches − good evening.

buenas tardes − good afternoon.

bueno − good.

capitán − military rank of Captain.

casita − a small building often used for family or guests located close to the main house.

chicken sancocho − chicken stew-like soup.

collective − the pitch control generally situated on the left side of the pilot's seat. The collective changes the pitch angle of all the main rotor blades, and as a result, the helicopter increases or decreases its total lift derived from the rotor.

Colegio Javier – Xavier College

Compagnie Universelle du Canal Interocéanique - The Universal Company of the Interoceanic Canal of Panama, created on October 20, 1880, by Ferdinand de Lesseps to build the Panama Canal.

conquistadores – Spanish conquerors of the New World in the 16th Century.

cuidado – look out.

cyclic – The cyclic is similar in appearance to a control stick in a conventional aircraft. The cyclic stick commonly rises from beneath the front of each pilot's seat. The cyclic is used to control the main rotor in order to change the helicopter's direction of movement. In a hover, the cyclic controls the movement of the helicopter forward, back, and laterally. During forward flight, the cyclic control inputs cause flight path changes. Left or right inputs cause the helicopter to roll into a turn in the desired direction. Forward and back inputs change the pitch attitude of the helicopter resulting in altitude changes (climbing or descending flight).

encantado – delighted.

Escudo – Gold escudos were introduced as early as 1535 and became the dominant coin in Spain, Portugal, and their colonies for centuries.

estadounidense – Americans from the United States.

estas bien – are you OK?

Fuerza Aérea Panameña – Panamanian Air Force.

finca – a rural property, farm, or ranch.

gracias – thank you.

hola – hello.

Madre de Dios – oh my God.

maldita sea – dammit.

matón – thug.

Mi Diario – a Spanish-language newspaper published in Panama.

mira – look.

morion – a helmet without visor, worn by Spanish soldiers in the 16th and 17th centuries.

no comprendo – I don't understand.

norteamericano – a citizen or resident of the United States, as distinguished from the peoples of Spanish- speaking America.

No sé – I don't know.

Oficina de Investigación de Accidentes Aéreos – The Office of Investigation of Air Accidents (OFINVAA) the investigating arm of the Panamanian Civil Aeronautics Authority. Roughly equivalent to the U.S. National Transportation Safety Board.

Panamá la Vieja – the remaining part of the original Panama City, destroyed in 1671 by the Welsh privateer Henry Morgan.

paraíso – paradise.

Parque nacional Camino de Cruces – *Camino de Cruces* national park. The *Camino de Cruces* Trail was originally used in the 16th and 17th centuries by the Spanish to transport gold taken from Peru by mule across the Isthmus of Panama on its way to Spain.

Parque nacional Soberanía – *Soberanía* National Park located near the banks of the Panama Canal in the provinces of Panamá and Colón, some 16 miles from Panama City. The park is popular with birdwatchers due to its abundance of bird species; some 525 bird species are found here.

profesor – professor.

sal de aquí – get out of here.

Sanctuario de Aves – bird sanctuary.

Señor – title or form of address for a Spanish-speaking man used like "Mister" in English.

Señora – title or form of address for a married Spanish-speaking lady used like "Mrs." or "Madam" in English.

Señorita – title or form of address for an unmarried Spanish-speaking lady used like "Miss" in English.

señoritas – unmarried ladies.

sí – yes.

siesta – short afternoon nap.

tío – uncle.

Turista Pensionado – Pensioned Tourist. A Panamania government visa designed for persons whose pension from a government entity or private corporation is $500 or more ($600 or more for a couple per month). The Pensionado Visa is granted indefinitely. It is an instant permanent residency program similar to a "Green Card" in the United States.

Universidad de Panamá – University of Panama

Volcán de Oro – Golden Volcano.

yuca frita – fried edible root of the cassava plant.

ACKNOWLEDGMENTS

The authors would like to thank several technical experts who contributed their knowledge and, in some cases, did original research to permit us to make every possible fact as accurate as needed to advance the story. These include Lt. Col. Brinn Colenda, USAF (Ret.), currently residing in Panama under the *Turista Pensionado* program. We also thank his wife, Lindy, for reviewing our use of the Spanish language.

Writing about an aircraft crash is a challenge. Neither of the authors is helicopter-rated, but we were able to obtain assistance from three former helicopter pilots: Teddy Adams—Army, Darcy Vernier—Marine Corps, and Bill Martin—Navy. Between the three of them and the authors' writing talents, we think we provided the reader with a very realistic chapter.

The history curator at the Albuquerque Museum, Deb Slaney, was most helpful in providing photos of *morions* in their collection and assistance in finding the right words to describe their construction. Members of a weekly veterans writing group at the Raymond G. Murphy VA Medical Center offered their suggestions. The venue provided the authors with an opportunity to read their work out loud.

Jasmine Tritten, LLC, did the five original hand-drawn illustrations used in this book (dead antbird, Fer-de-Lance, metal trunk corner protector, Spanish gold escudo coin, Spanish *morion* helmet). Ownership of this original artwork was transferred to Sandi Hoover, LLC.

Two photographs used in this book are in the public domain. The Bell 47-OH-13 can be found at: https://commons.wikimedia.org/wiki/File:Bell_47-OH-13_inflight_bw.jpg. The coat of arms of *Panamá la Vieja* is located at: https://commons.wikimedia.org/wiki/File:84-Arms_of_the_Old_City_of_Panama.jpg with fair use policy posted at: http://shorturl.at/asvN1

The authors wish to thank the judges and staff involved with the New Mexico Press Women 2021 Communications Contest and the National Federation of Press Women 2021 Professional Communications Contest. *Panama's Gold* was awarded First Place in the category of Fiction for Adult Readers, Novellas (40,000 words or fewer) by New Mexico and it went on to win a Second Place in the national contest. Thanks to Sydnie Beaupré for including *Panama's Gold* as a contribution to a charity fundraiser in the anthology *Meltingpot: You are not alone*, Sydnie Beaupré, ed.; 1st Edition (October 13, 2020) https://www.amazon.com/Mltingpot-You-are-not-alone-ebook/dp/B08DL4K2V5

Thanks is also given to Kathy Hopkins, retired English teacher and current volunteer facilitator at the veterans writing group at the Raymond G. Murphy VA Medical Center in Albuquerque, New Mexico.

Finally, our thanks to our fellow members of the Corrales Writing Group for their insightful critiques—Chris Allen, John Atkins, Maureen Cooke, Tom Neiman, and Pat Walkow—and our spouses bear the brunt of reading the first drafts—Richard Hoover and Jasmine Tritten.

ABOUT THE AUTHORS

Sandi Hoover

Sandi has always been fascinated by animals, plants, and birds. Her childhood behind-the-scenes experiences during Summer Zoo School at the San Diego Zoo reinforced her enthusiasm. She spent her working career as executive director of the Houston Audubon Society and then the Bayou Preservation Association, both active conservation non-profit organizations. While those positions led to interesting activities, her writing was specific and pragmatic. There was no humor or fiction involved in position papers and environmental statements. Before joining the Corrales Writing

Group, her avocational writing was confined to personal travel journals and descriptive letters to family and friends, plus the occasional article for local newsletters. Since procrastination is easy —seemingly, only deadlines prompt action—joining the Corrales Writing Group has demanded the discipline of writing on a regular basis. Learning the craft of writing in a more formal way through presentation, followed by critique from this trusted group of friends, has provided a safe place to learn new skills and grow as an author.

A birder and naturalist, she enjoys watching and analyzing wildlife's behavior, trying to understand how they fulfill their basic needs. Her writings frequently reflect her interest in the natural world. Indulging her curiosity about nature has inspired trips to experience wilderness firsthand. From King Eiders in Barrow, Alaska, to King Penguins on South Georgia Island, seeing animals in their natural habitat has been a life-long pursuit. She still gazes out her office window or pets her cat (always kept safely indoors) instead of writing.

Jim Tritten

After a forty-four-year career with the Department of Defense, Jim retired, including duty as a carrier-based naval aviator. He holds advanced degrees from the University of Southern California and formerly served as a faculty member and National Security Affairs department chair at the Naval Postgraduate School. Dr. Tritten's publications have won him fifty-nine writing awards, including the Alfred Thayer Mahan Award from the Navy League of the U.S. He has published twelve books and over four hundred chapters, short stories, essays, articles, and government technical reports. Jim was a frequent speaker at many military, arms control, and international conferences and has seen his work translated into Russian, French, Spanish, and Portuguese.